More Praise for *Coup de Foudre*

"Almost my ideal of what the short story collection can do. The pieces are sufficiently different in terms of style and form that the reader never knows what to expect next—gimlet-eyed realism, creepy, surreal fables, satire, Chandler-esque obfuscated epiphanies or Borgesian parables." —***The Scotsman***

"Ken Kalfus's story, *Coup de Foudre*, is a brilliant fictional account of the incident [in which an international banking official was charged with sexually assaulting a hotel maid], framed as a cringe-making letter of apology." —***The Globe and Mail***

"In the title novella, Kalfus . . . riffs entertainingly on the outlaw sexual proclivities of a financial titan." —***The Forward***

"One of my best books this year." —**Jenni Russell, *The Times***

"[*Coup de Foudre*] showcases a dazzling versatility of style and imagination . . . devotees and newcomers alike will be richly rewarded by the author's impressive display here of rhetorical inventiveness and ingenious ideas." —***Booklist***

"Well-written . . . Accomplished and often [gives] great insight into the curious ways of people." —***Kirkus Reviews***

"Kalfus's stories . . . roll in like thunder . . . Together they create a pensive and wistful atmosphere. Kalfus blends science and philosophy to create whimsical, off-kilter worlds only slightly different from our own and in which entire universes are born—slanted but familiar. A playful and poignant collection of fiction that masterfully toes the line between comic and tragic." —***Shelf Awareness***

"Provocative explorations into contemporary culture." —***BookReporter.com***

"Psychologically brilliant." —***New Statesman***

"Clever . . . Kalfus captures [his worlds] with dry wit and polished style, gliding from piece to piece and skewering everyone from the powerful to the powerless." —***The Harvard Crimson***

"*Coup de Foudre*, the novella which forms the centerpiece of his most recent collection of short fiction, is a coruscating example of [Kalfus'] gutsiness and high literary ambition . . . This is an intelligent and very rewarding collection of short stories, with a brilliant flagship novella." —***Cleaver Magazine***

"Can you call a Guggenheim Fellow and a National Book Award Finalist unheralded? Maybe not, but underheralded Ken Kalfus most certainly is. With *Coup de Foudre*, he's written as varied and exciting a collection as any you're likely to find, a wild array of stories and novellas made whole by the artfulness of his prose, the bravery of his tactics, and the empathy and honesty of his gaze." **—Kevin Brockmeier, author of *The Illumination***

"Ken Kalfus keeps you teetering between 'this is weird' and 'exactly right!' The strange worlds he brilliantly creates are oddly familiar and make you laugh and think and hope for more. He is an original with the gift of getting inside people." **—Mark Kurlansky, author of *City Beasts***

"Ken Kalfus's exuberant fictions about scamps, fumblers, and modern day rogues comes as a relief—so *this* is how they think. Kalfus cracks the human personality code with *Coup de Foudre*. Yet another of the author's literary accomplishments, chock-full of clear-eyed portraits in an entertaining and experimental vein." —**Amity Gaige, author of *Schroder***

"It is impossible to stay detached from a Ken Kalfus story. No matter how unsettling their predicaments, the characters in this striking collection are rendered so fully and precisely that we can feel the force of their desires and understand their panic and confusion. Whether the subject is sexual assault, an eerie curse cast on a community, the act of reading, or even gingivitis, these fictions are infused with the force of lived experience." **—Joanna Scott, author of *De Potter's Grand Tour***

"*Coupe de Foudre* is a riveting feat of imagination." **—Christine Sneed, author of *Paris, He Said***

"A meticulous exploration of the inner life of a rich powerful white late-middle-aged internationally urbane multilingual Viagra-mainlining sex addict politician." ***—The Buffalo News***

"This latest collection of groundbreaking short fiction is as inventive as fans of Ken's work will expect." **—BroadwayWorld.com**

"[With] stories that range from funny to farcical . . . it's a treat for those unafraid to question conventional thinking." ***—Philly Voice***

BY THE SAME AUTHOR

NOVELS

Equilateral

A Disorder Peculiar to the Country

The Commissariat of Enlightenment

STORIES

Pu-239 and Other Russian Fantasies

Thirst

Coup de Foudre

A NOVELLA AND STORIES

KEN KALFUS

B L O O M S B U R Y
NEW YORK • LONDON • OXFORD • NEW DELHI • SYDNEY

Bloomsbury USA
An imprint of Bloomsbury Publishing Plc

1385 Broadway
New York
NY 10018
USA

50 Bedford Square
London
WC1B 3DP
UK

www.bloomsbury.com

First published 2015
This paperback edition published 2016

Versions of these stories previously appeared in the following publications: "Coup de Foudre" and "The Moment They Were Waiting For" in *Harper's*; "In Borges' Library" in *Pulpsmith*; " 'City of Spies' " in *Columbia*; "Square Paul-Painlevé" in *Swissair Gazette*; "Professor Arecibo" and "The Un-" in *AGNI*; "Instructions for My Literary Executors" in *Salon*; "Mercury" in the *Paris Review*; "The Moment They Were Waiting For," "Professor Arecibo," and "The Un-" were published in a limited-edition chapbook, *Three Stories*, by Madras Press.

The author wishes to thank the Ucross Foundation for a productive residency while working on this book.

ISBN: HB: 978-1-62040-085-2
ePub: 978-1-62040-086-9
PB: 978-1-63286-380-5

LIBRARY OF CONGRESS CATALOGING-IN-PUBLICATION DATA

Kalfus, Ken.
[Short stories. Selections]
Coup de foudre: a novella and stories / Ken Kalfus.—First U.S. edition.
pages ; cm
ISBN 978-1-62040-085-2 (hardcover) 978-1-62040-086-9 (ebook)
I. Title.
PS3561.A416524A6 2015
813'.54—dc23
2014043596

2 4 6 8 10 9 7 5 3 1

Typeset by RefineCatch Ltd, Bungay, Suffolk
Printed and bound in the U.S.A by Sheridan

For Inga and Sky

Some innocents 'scape not the thunderbolt.

—*Antony and Cleopatra*, act II, scene 5

CONTENTS

Part I

Coup de Foudre

COUP DE FOUDRE

ONE

Mariama, you'll never read this letter: if I sent it, our civil settlement would be invalidated and the district attorney would reopen the criminal case. I have no reason to send it, because I will never ask for your forgiveness. My offense was too great. I got away with it. I'm pleased to remain at liberty. Plus they say you're illiterate. Yet we commonly recognize that some moral benefit lies in acknowledging our errors, even privately, in order to do penance and seek correction in our behavior. The more truthfully and fully and exactingly we do our accounting, the greater the value. As usual, then, it transpires that I'm acting on my own behalf.

If I could communicate with you, my principal intention would be to persuade you that I'm not a madman, though I understand it's not obvious that I'm *not* a madman (and even writing this unsendable letter testifies against my sanity). I concede that my mind is not right these days, these days of disgrace. My mind was certainly not right at the time of our encounter. Although I was alert to what I was doing, I was also trapped within some kind of mental tunnel in which I was unable to perceive the outer world, or the constraints that usually apply to human relations. I had been locked in this tunnel—less metaphorically, a highly excitable and distracted state of mind—for the past several days, my thoughts careening against the passageway's frictionless walls from one data point related to international finance to the next. Also, from woman to woman. I cannot, however, plead that I was not myself. The more closely I recall those actions and circumstances, the more convinced I am that in those terrible minutes my true character emerged. This is the character that would have been suppressed, or crushed or strangled or decapitated, the moment I declared my candidacy.

Before those minutes, Mariama, you were not one of the tens of millions of people around the world for whom the name David Lèon Landau signified financial brilliance in the service of the public. After you were told who I was, later that day, the name still meant nothing to you, though years ago I was involved in writing the terms of the low-interest bond issue that secured a water treatment plant in Guinea's Fouta Djallon highlands, not far from your place of birth. I like to think that your lips were once refreshed by cool water gurgling from the village's communal pipe, and that you sipped it thirstily and with pleasure. Some may have spilled from the sides of your mouth. You may have even reflected at the time on the miracle of the liquid's animating power and plenitude.

Power and plenitude: in the minutes before our encounter I was taking a shower, which was set to full force and very hot, fully steaming the wildly oversize New York hotel bathroom. The shower's intensity did nothing to mitigate my erection, which was fueled by an overreliance on Viagra the night before and the night before that (I will avoid inflicting my erections on you any further, except when unavoidable). I wasn't thinking of sex. Rather, I was brooding about the set of problems that seemed to define my life that morning. Chief among them was the European debt crisis and my crucial appointment with the refractory German chancellor the next day. I was also alarmed about a text message I had received that morning from a friend in Paris, suggesting that my political opponents had gained access to my e-mails. Only two days earlier, in Washington, D.C., another friend had delivered an urgent warning that I was being spied on by French intelligence—a warning, we learned later, that was clandestinely recorded. I turned my face into the water as if it were a liberating scour.

TWO

If you've taken an interest in the particulars of your own legal case (and you may not have), you will know that on the Thursday night before our encounter I attended what the papers have termed a "libertine party," at the W hotel in Washington with three of my friends and a few women. After the women left, we returned to the suite's dining room, where the dinner dishes were not yet cleared, and compared notes over a rare bottle of calvados, distilled in 1865 and bottled in 1912. The brandy, which had crossed the Atlantic three times, was a postcoital custom, a token of our friendship and our common pursuit. We spoke little, making mostly quiet comments about what we had shared. We raised glasses to the distinct qualities of the women we had been with: the infectious laugh of one, another's globular behind. With good humor, alacrity, and sometimes astounding invention, the women had performed several preliminary sex acts with us and among themselves, before accepting us as lovers somewhere within the suite's tenebrous rooms and alcoves. More than a hundred apples had gone into the wide-hipped brown bottle; the apples were as tart and fresh as if they had just been picked.

My friend Philippe, a regional police commissioner in France, tilted his empty glass toward the bottle, which remained on the table in front of the sofa, and said, "We should finish it now."

Another friend, Marc, objected, "There's enough for Rio."

Philippe allowed Marc's point to stand, but I guessed his baleful meaning. I rose from the couch, tightened the hotel robe around my girth, and walked to the window that looked out onto the memorial to General Washington. The capital seemed especially sterile to me now, sterile and pompous, and, like the obelisk, overly obvious. I wished Philippe hadn't said anything. Despite the expense (mostly Marc's) and the intricate arrangements (especially after we moved the party to D.C.), the thousands of miles several of us had flown to come here, the fineness of the meal, and the fabulousness of the women, these evenings were like delicate flowers, every petal trembling before the ardent touch.

Later, after Marc and our other companion, Josef, were gone, Philippe remained in the corner wing chair, bare-chested, an empty tumbler in hand. "You have too many enemies," he said. "You're about to have many more."

I went again to the window. I wished I could throw it open, lean out, and get a lungful of American air, but it was sealed.

"They're watching you, David. Whatever you do, whoever you're with. Once you declare, it'll be worse."

"I know, they're already digging under every rock. *Figaro. Le Point.*"

"The press is a nuisance, but you should worry about Sarkozy. He's looking for every edge. I hear that he has people in the DCRI, or the DCRI has people it can call on for him. It's becoming dangerous, and not only for you. Everything's at stake now. We have to stop."

The DCRI is the Direction Centrale du Renseignement Intérieur, the French domestic intelligence service. As a former government minister, I was aware of the agency's surveillance capabilities, and I also knew the strict legal prohibitions against using them for political purposes. But Sarkozy is another Nixon. Those prohibitions would mean nothing to him.

I gazed down at the illuminated, pink-and-white chessboard plaza in front of the Department of the Treasury, across from the hotel. I had passed over those tiles only a few hours previously, for my appointment with the undersecretary. We had commiserated over the grim European numbers, aware that several lines of power ran, crackling, through his office, which looked out on a garden, in which the geraniums and roses were in full Maytime bloom, and that this power was at our disposal if only we had the courage to use it. The power was still there tonight. I had sent a preliminary proposal to the treasury secretary, Timothy Geithner.

"It was a lovely evening though, wasn't it, Philippe? Those new girls were splendid. I won't ask you where you found them. Very compassionate. Giselle has this little maneuver, a flick of the pelvis at the right moment . . . Exquisite. How does one learn that move? How is the technique transmitted from one generation of chicks to the next? I presume they don't get it from their mothers. And the kitchen was very decent tonight, even if they had to be instructed."

"Yes," Philippe said, knowing he would get no further with me now and preferring to share the moment. He had already told me that he came three times with Lucy, the miracle girl. Whatever was going to happen, in the next month or the following year, this was a very fine moment. Of course, I haven't seen Philippe since then, and probably never will again.

THREE

Few downfalls in public life have been as well documented as my own. Electronic keycards recorded every time the door to my New York hotel suite was opened from the corridor and by whom, whether guest or staff member. Security cameras in the lobby, corridors, and employee areas tracked the movements of every person within the building.

In those years when I strode the world stage, I always carried with me several cell phones in various states of discharge; the time and duration of each phone call made from them were logged with their service providers. My BlackBerry usage would prove to be of particular interest. The timeline of my descent has been established right down to the second of impact. I have it before me, along with several books and investigative articles on the case and a layout of the hotel suite.

Omissions in the record remain, however, leaving troublesome questions about the events of the day. The keycards don't record when individuals *leave* hotel rooms, for example. If the New York district attorney had succeeded in bringing the case against me to trial, most of these omissions would have been addressed, either by the prosecution or by my defense. Your testimony would have been pitted against my own. A new narrative would have emerged, giving each actor in the drama sensibility and motive. The criminal case collapsed because of doubts cast on your credibility that were mostly related to certain falsehoods filed in your immigration papers years ago, not to our sexual encounter. So the mysteries are still here, stalking me in the underfurnished rooms of my bachelor flat.

No one contests that there was a sexual encounter: my semen was identified on your uniform top and mixed in with the saliva that you spat onto the carpet. Yet I was prepared to argue in court that our sex was consensual—even if we had never before met, even though our entire romantic affair, from the first hello to the first stirrings of desire, the rites of courtship, the sexual act itself, and the sweet regretful murmurs of farewell, had to be encompassed within minutes.

After my arrest for sexual assault, I was held for four days in Rikers Island, and then under house arrest in New York for more than a month. Once the district attorney saw that he wouldn't win his case against my best-in-the-business defense team, I was free to leave the States—but with my job lost, my candidacy undeclared, and my reputation wrecked. My wife would shortly leave me, *quelle surprise*. Your lawyers filed a civil suit. We've now negotiated a settlement that will depend on both sides keeping silent about what really happened that day in the presidential suite of the New York Sofitel.

So the truth remains unvoiced and legally unvoiceable. If your lawyers or the DA knew that I was composing this account privately, my hard drive would be subpoenaed through the French courts. The civil settlement would fall apart. The criminal case would be reopened. Yet as dangerous as this confession may be to my freedom, I'm compelled to sit myself before this laptop and let the words fall like tears upon the keyboard. Without the construction of a narrative that explains what I did to you and what I did to myself, I could very well lose my mind.

FOUR

The thought that everything depended on Angela Merkel reverberated across the bright hours of the morning after the Washington sex party, Friday. I went to my office to study the latest figures from Greece. They were appalling figures, promising severe hardship to real people. I exchanged phone calls with finance officials and private economists on three continents. Everyone was looking at the same fateful numbers and depositing them into ever-more-esoteric equations. Contagion was probable: Italy, Spain, and Portugal were at immediate risk, and not even France was safe. I had virtually begged Angela to see me on Sunday. We needed to show the markets something before they opened on Monday. "Chancellor, please. We've come up with a plan. It's effective, it's comprehensive, and it's politically palatable." She had refused at first, insisting that Sunday was the day she reserved for her personal life.

Her personal life. This was an abdication of power. Millions of personal lives would be ruined if the correct measures were not taken within the next few days. I scorned her fear, her manifold hesitancies, and her sluggishness, which I had come to know well, almost intimately. She was like a peasant farmer, some *Kleinbäuerin*, guarding her stash of 6 percent unemployment and her 3.1 percent bond yield in the cellar while famine ravaged the land. If she would only bring her potatoes to market . . . Of course I didn't tell her the inconvenience I had gone to, forced to move up the sex party a day and from New York to Washington, in order to accommodate our Sunday appointment.

The only way forward was for Europe to buy the crappy Greek debt; the figures involved were relatively small, sixty billion euros, about the same as Lower Saxony's direct indebtedness. Greece's creditors would have to take a haircut, but they'd survive. Once the Eurobond structure was established, investors would be reassured: money was still to be made in Europe.

Angela would claim the Bundesrepublik's constitution forbids the German government from lending beyond parliamentary control, but there were ways to get around that. I had studied the relevant articles and consulted with friends in the Berlin judiciary. I had spoken, behind her back, with the relevant power brokers in her own party. I knew I could bring the banks on board and sell it to the other European leaders. Everything was manageable, as soon as that stolid, dreary woman was ready to exercise the power with which she had been invested.

A car took me to Reagan Airport as I beat down a rising tide of anger. Everything was manageable and everyone made everything hard. Sarkozy would try to smash my head in even as he took credit for the plan. The lazy, lying Greeks would squeal at austerity while I saved them from privation. They'd send thugs out onto the streets. The IMF's directors were ready to pounce if anything went wrong. Angela would put on her stern face, show resistance and anger, and who knew what kind of *Ossi* passive aggression. She would have to be romanced.

Meanwhile, even my friends were reining me in, trying to refashion me as a conventional political candidate, captive to conventional sentiment. What to say. Where to appear. Which gimcrack ring to kiss on the wrinkled hand of which constipated fool. Philippe was right of course, I knew we'd have to stop getting together once the campaign began. Once I declared—then I would no longer belong to myself. I would belong to the Party and certain proprieties would have to be observed.

If I declared . . . A part of me sought the presidency as I have sought other offices, only because I knew I was the best person for it. Urgent measures had to be taken for France's future, and for Europe's; I would assume the commitment to achieve them. That was my strength. I recognized that most men shunned challenges and difficulties: I rushed to them. Other men minimized risks: I coolly weighed them against what could be achieved. They feared being shackled by responsibility. But for a man such as myself responsibility was not a restriction: it was the key to personal freedom. Responsibility gave me license to exercise my intelligence, my resolve, and my talents of persuasion. I could act where others would not.

That was on one hand; the other hand grasped at a multitude of slippery ambiguities. My actions in the next twenty-four hours would suggest to many that I never wanted the presidency at all.

At Reagan, passing through check-in and security, I was nearly vibrating with conflicting aspirations. As if Terminal B were an enormous vagina, slick and firm—pardon me, Mariama, but that was the image that came to mind—I was surrounded by womanhood: travelers, busty TSA cops, and, moving in small packs, tight-skirted stewardesses, who effected a twinge in my lower groin area no less than their grandmothers did on my first airplane flight, to Nice on a family vacation when I was nine years of age. At the security gate women were removing their shoes, slipping or even hopping out of them no differently than they might have in the bedroom. I couldn't help but believe, for a moment at least, that they were doing it for me. I watched. At a newsstand after I was screened, I stopped near a blonde in a long, flowing black dress. She squatted, balancing on the balls of her feet, at a lower magazine rack where the art magazines were kept. Her breasts surged from the top of her low neckline. I circled around to catch a better view and found myself in front of men's pornography—something I have no use for, by the way.

As I approached my gate, I spied another woman, in a tight, red sheath dress and matching heels, and wanted her, and knew, as I knew many things, that I could have her. Her dress stopped not quite midthigh. She milled with the other passengers waiting for their rows to be called. First class was boarding now, but I didn't join the queue. I couldn't see her face. I didn't know whether she was pretty or plain, and when I reached the waiting area, she shifted her stance and turned her head, as if deliberately defending against my scrutiny. There wasn't enough time to invite her for a drink in the Delta Sky Club. Unless of course I convinced her, with the promise of a first-class upgrade, to catch the next flight.

The thought tormented me: I was on a tight schedule. I was getting into New York late and meeting my friend Claudette for dinner. I had some phone appointments Saturday morning and lunch with my daughter at noon, and then I had to catch the 4:40 flight to Paris. From Paris on Sunday, after stopping home to see my wife, I was flying on to Berlin. I did not need any entanglements right now. The girl was still appealing, though. That turn away from me, on her pretty red heels, showing the curve of her delicate bottom, could have been an act of deliberate coquetry. I loved that. You must wonder how I could be so smart and yet think so recklessly.

This was, however, exactly the man I was, the man I am today, the man who would save the European economy and the man who wanted to fuck this woman silly—or at least have her masturbate him in first class, under a first-class blanket, as a giggling Filipina in tight stonewashed jeans had once kindly obliged him, from Vienna to Amsterdam. And this man—me!—was getting older: I was sixty-two, conventionally, restrictively, thought to be too old for these passions and these games, but I would age only further, and these pleasures would further recede from my embrace. I was surrounded by those who wished to rush deprivations at me: my wife, my sister, my (former) doctor, who demanded that I cut back my consumption of salt. I decided to approach the woman. Success often depends less on good judgment than on one's decisiveness.

Not every man has my determination, but every man is no less concupiscent, whether he's married or single, getting it regularly or not. He may be the perspiring comb-over with a somber, heavy-lidded demeanor, or the goofy, bucktoothed busboy whose bedroom is postered with images of footballers, or the wise, soft-spoken rabbi, or the hideously maimed war veteran. Every one of those men who are heterosexual is watching you and your sisters, Mariama, surreptitiously or candidly, judging the outline of a breast and then extrapolating, or assessing a tush, an ankle, or a pair of full, vermilion lips. The turn of a head and its momentary reveal of a long, slender neck give us a deep and abiding pleasure, regardless of what happens next. Count on it.

The woman in the red sheath was less than thirty feet away, but other passengers and their carry-ons stood between us, almost deliberately, I thought. I picked my way around them, nearly tripping over some toddler of indeterminate sex. The woman remained beyond my reach. The plane's back rows were called and the passengers frantically assembled themselves into a sloppy queue. I was blocked again. The woman went through the gate and vanished into coach without showing her face.

I waited at the back of the line, sullenly handed over my boarding pass, and took my seat within a row of gray American suits. I looked around. A lady my own age occupied the aisle seat two rows ahead, nothing special, and the stewardesses were strictly shuttle-class.

FIVE

I concede that not every man is as preoccupied as I was, and I'm not always this way: the sexual restlessness rises and subsides from time to time. I can only speculate about what triggers it, or why this peculiar temper was so overwhelming that weekend. The previous night's revels were still fresh in my mind, of course. My sorrow at their conclusion was fresh too, as was the awareness that they might never be repeated. Philippe's cautions weighed on me. So did Angela's skittishness about the Sunday meeting. In truth, she hadn't wished to see me at all.

When the plane landed at JFK, I startled from an old man's uneasy half doze, momentarily forgetting the name of the city that was my destination. I took my bag and briefcase and disembarked with the other first-class passengers, and then I recalled the girl in the red sheath dress. A girl like that, or as I imagined her to be, with those heels: certainly she was headed into Manhattan. I would invite her to share my cab. I stopped, positioned myself nearly at the lip of the uniformly beige tunnel, and adopted a roguish smile, without gazing directly at the passengers who exited the plane. I didn't want the woman to be aware, from too far down the tunnel, that I was waiting for her. I needed to retain an element of surprise; I also wished to avoid seeming predatory.

A number of attractive women came out of the plane, several of them preoccupied with their wheeled bags. She wasn't among them. They didn't take note of the distinguished European man who stood off to the side. I waited patiently, continuing to avert my eyes. The flow of passengers diminished to a trickle. I began to feel foolish. My roguish smile froze. A stewardess finally escorted the last travelers from the cabin, two elderly men. I had missed the woman. She must have changed in the lavatory while we were en route, wiggling out of her dress, for reasons that were entirely her own. I turned away. Annoyed at the deception, I strode with purpose into the terminal.

As consolation I lingered for a few moments over the thought of that wiggle.

The lost opportunity nagged at me all the way into the city, even though I was aware how slender an opportunity it had been, probably. She could have rebuffed me. Someone could have been waiting for her at the airport. She could have been going to Brooklyn. Every possibility, every notion, was now piling up against the others like an accident on a fast highway. I would have to stay focused, I told myself vaguely. I would have to keep faith with my most important task, preparing for my Sunday meeting with Angela Merkel.

The resolve lasted only a minute after my taxi deposited me at the Sofitel, where you had already gone home for the day. When I entered the cool, subtly lit lobby, I was immediately aware that it was populated by beautiful women, all of them made-up and coiffed like Hollywood stars. Some were evidently guests, lounging cinematically on the overplush upholstery. Others wore crisp black uniforms, their hair tied back severely, and they glided with no less elegance across the marble inlaid floor. But now, reflecting on my arrival, I also recall one or two crew-cut, ear-pieced men in the shadows, witnessing my entrance. They didn't look like bellboys.

"Monsieur Landau."

The VIP concierge was waiting for me, beaming. I suppose you know her. With a discretion perfected over decades, I acquired her first name from the enameled bijou pinned a few inches north-northwest of her pert right breast. Her left seemed quite pert too, by the way.

"Adele," I said.

"We're pleased to see you again," she said, dimpling. After I checked in, she offered to show me to my room.

I was aware that this courtesy was obligatory, but it could have been something else too. In the course of our noiseless, lubricated ascent to the twenty-eighth floor, I let her know she was being appraised. She smiled in return, showing those winsome dimples again, and I thought to myself, a possibility.

"I was last here in March," I said.

"I recall."

"That you recall makes me inordinately, inappropriately happy."

But when we arrived at my floor and entered the so-called presidential suite, the woman proved elusive. She walked me through the living room, the dining room, the kitchen, and the bedroom and demonstrated the function of the large-screen television, and every time I tried to block her, she passed around me as if I were not there at all. Before I could close the door to the suite, she wished me a pleasant stay and turned on her heels, without giving away the slightest suggestion of haste. This too was a practiced skill.

I wondered if there was significance in her recollection of my last visit. The room service or housekeeping staff may have talked. Mariama, you may have heard certain rumors too, or started them, if you were the housekeeper assigned to clean the suite. That rainy March morning, even with the women gone, enough underthings had been left behind to stock a small boutique. I recalled now that here in the dining room, not once getting up from her knees, Claudette had fellated three of us, one right after the other.

I checked my messages, washed up, and looked at my messages again. Queries flooded my in-box from finance ministries all over the world. I answered the most urgent of them with assurances that I would address every issue in Berlin.

Now I was alone in a suite that had been fashioned for sex: a king-size bed, two couches, a bar, plush rugs, and a view of Manhattan that warmed the loins. It was early evening. The city's skyscrapers were still illuminated within the embers of the fading workweek. The two rivers, slightly different shades of slate blue, extended on either side of me, specked by tiny tugs and ferries. That's what you get for $3,000. We had planned a leisurely, long-weekend bacchanal here, but then the crisis intervened. Once our party was moved to D.C., I could have canceled the reservation and stayed in a less expensive room or simply not come to New York. I hadn't because I never like to give up the potential for sex.

I remembered that the receptionist who'd checked me in was not half-bad, though I can't say in what way, or anything else about her. Despite my keen appreciation of the feminine form, I sometimes fail to recall the physical characteristics of the women I encounter in the course of a day, not even those I wish to have sex with or actually do have sex with. When I meet a woman, it's the idea of her, specifically her carnal essence, and not her transient features, that lodges in my mind. I can't tell you the most recent cut of my wife's hair, long or short, bangs or no bangs, or the haircut before that, as stylish as it may have been.

I called down and invited the young lady to my suite for a glass of wine. Room service was offering a 2003 Pauillac. She said, thank you, but that it wouldn't be possible. She offered no further explanation. I returned the receiver to its cradle as gently as I could.

Claudette couldn't meet me until ten. She lived a complicated life, of which I was not the most tangled complication, at least not at that time. She had a husband in Paris, older than me and physically abusive, with whom she holidayed in Miami every winter. He knew about me; the American boyfriend, also married, was clueless. Her sister in Lyon was chronically in debt. Claudette herself was afflicted by some irregular immigration status, which I could have remedied with a single phone call, but she declined my help. Perhaps she feared that she would have had to disclose further complications. I'll never learn now what they were. Sweet, quick-witted, sperm-hungry Claudette: I haven't spoken to her either since that weekend.

I descended to the lobby, ignoring the receptionist and the concierge, who would both later report my advances to investigators, and went into the street, into the lusty New York springtime. It was eight P.M. and the sidewalks coursed with alluring women of all races. They met my searching eyes. Some were unaccompanied. I had no plan for these hours, but every moment of eye contact, every wordless exchange, provoked another review of possible strategies and tactics.

I felt completely at home. I'm one of the tens of millions of people, including nearly every Parisian, who live outside New York and consider ourselves New Yorkers, either because of time spent here or familiarity with the city from films and books or simply because we embrace its spirit of cosmopolitan, mercantilistic, street-smart, class-jumping, opportunity-seeking liberty. We keep MetroCards in our wallets. We support the Yankees. We defend our favorite West Village restaurants, even if they closed fifteen years ago.

My whereabouts from eight until early Saturday morning would remain undiscovered by the prosecutor, who may not have been interested in them anyway. They were, for me, hours of a rather typical New York evening. I meandered, my turn at each corner dependent on the direction of the WALK sign. I bought a hot dog with sauerkraut and relish from a vendor at a pushcart. I gave directions to a young backpacker stopped in the middle of pedestrian traffic, her map in hand. Tearing off a piece of the frank, I smiled appreciatively at two older women in short spring coats, meeting their husbands I guess, well made up for their Friday-night dates. Their smiles in return were blindingly full toothed. I was casting my line, mostly out of restlessness, knowing that I would be seeing Claudette soon enough, yet also keen to determine what else was within range of my barbed hook.

After a while my random walk brought me to the sidewalk outside a scarf store, the bright colors and soft textures of its merchandise beckoning my attention. I peered through the glass door at the three young women inside. The store owner clearly had a specific taste in girls—leggy, angular, small in the chest, and long-necked—or perhaps these are the physical types of women that most vigorously suggest the need for a scarf. I'm sure someone has done a study. Tonight I was the only customer and each salesgirl smiled at me in her own way: the first with a smirky, crooked turn of her mouth, the second with pursed lips, the third with a toss of her head. Each smile made its own promise.

I know something about scarves, and in fact the night before we had used a couple to tie down one of the new girls. She had squealed like a teenager, which she may have been. Now I walked slowly by the vitrines, ignoring the more modestly priced items on display outside them.

"Good evening, sir!"

The greeting emerged from the pursed lips, which were slightly chapped. The gamine's pixieish, close-cropped hair was jet-black and her eyes were wide and alert.

"And to you, my dear. It's a splendid evening. Almost too splendid to be shopping for a scarf. I wonder why I came in."

"Are you looking for something specific?"

I caught her eye and held it for some time.

“Yes, I certainly am.”

She didn’t flinch or blush, to her credit.

I paused for a few moments, letting her further consider what I might be looking for, and then I said, “Something in a square silk twill, dip-dyed. Hermès or Lanvin, perhaps.”

“Do you have a particular color in mind?”

“No,” I said, and then added in a murmur, “something *rich*.”

With deft, careful movements, she removed several scarves, which I asked her to model. She took the time to drape the fabrics neatly around her neck and fold them, one way and then another. The other salesgirls watched us, politely removed. My girl showed me a scarf the color of a blood orange; another was like the purpling of low clouds at sunset. She turned so that I could see them—*her*—from every angle, each pose languorous and beguiling. The last scarf, a rich electric blue precisely the same color as her lacquered nails, appeared to ignite a cool glow in her eyes. She smiled, knowing she looked very fine and knowing that I appreciated her fineness.

“Do you like it?” I asked.

“It’s lovely,” she agreed, checking a mirror, and then she grinned, her vanity winning out over her reserve. This smile was more attractive than the pursed lips with which she welcomed the shop’s customers.

"Please wrap it then."

Her long fingers manipulated the fabric and tissue. The scarf went into the box folded as crisply as a newly engraved banknote. Under my steady gaze she may have been slowly comprehending, half in embarrassment, for whom the scarf was intended.

She gave me the bill, for $410. I barely looked at it before handing over my AmEx Centurion, the anodized-titanium Black Card, an advertisement for sexual prowess if there ever was one.

"I suppose your shop will close shortly," I said, while she ran the card through. Shopgirls are usually impressed with the Black Card or made anxious by it. Often they have never seen one before or may not know they exist. They call their supervisors. This girl made no sign of surprise. She may have been preoccupied by the meaning of the scarf. Would she refuse it? Would she be enticed? "I also suppose that at the end of a long day even the most charming and attractive sales associate will require a drink."

A woman balances herself on a precipice, a football, a tightrope, or a rickety chair. She may or may not decide to fall.

"That's a good guess," she said hesitantly. Now she gave the name embossed on the card a closer look. "You're David Lèon Landau! Of course! I should have recognized you."

"You should have?" I signed the receipt.

"I'm studying at NYU's Stern School, in the core business program with a concentration in finance. It's a terrific program, with a global-affairs component. We talk about Greece every morning. I bet you do too."

"That's also a good guess," I said, taken aback by the turn in the conversation.

"I wouldn't count on the Germans. Merkel's very sensitive to public opinion, especially after losing the state election in Baden-Württemberg. I can tell you right now, she won't bail out the Greeks."

"That's not what we're asking her to do," I countered somewhat defensively. Our critics would have called the proposal a bailout. Our success would have depended on defining the plan as something entirely different.

"She's already facing a constitutional challenge for last year's rescue package," the girl said. "She's defending credit guarantees to Ireland and Portugal and has to be worried about Spanish bond rates. Meanwhile, Greece isn't technically excluded from the capital markets yet. Athens can use the time to think about the consequences of leaving the euro."

By confirming that I would be making a proposal, I had already told the shopgirl more than what had been reported by the press.

"Those are significant consequences, for Germany and the world. All the more reason to devise a comprehensive solution," I said, precisely what I intended to tell Angela, in precisely that same soft, stern voice. The girl wasn't buying it. I offered my hand coolly. "I'm very pleased to meet you. Good luck with your studies."

"Thank you," she said, indifferent to having lost the drink and the scarf in the heat of macroeconomic analysis. She was a hard, bright young woman and fully self-possessed, never a real prospect. She had her own agenda. Adopting a bloodless professional register, she added, "Please allow me to send you my curriculum vitae. Next month I get my bachelor of science with honors. I'm looking for a position in an international lending institution."

We exchanged business cards and I left the shop with the scarf in a box in a little white shopping bag. I went to the restaurant where I was to meet Claudette, the girl's speech weighing on me.

SIX

Claudette finally arrived a little before ten, and I was not the only man at the bar riveted by her entrance, in heels and a sheer black micro. I gaze at her now. From the wreckage of my career, with its abandoned file cabinets and confiscated desktop computers, I've managed to rescue a series of photographs that I can study and savor in my solitude, spread across my dining-room table. They show Claudette in different states of undress, some of them on her own, some with a variety of sexual partners, some at the Sofitel. Now we kissed softly on the lips, like an old married couple.

"Sorry I'm so late," she said. "Michael's wife had to go in for treatment and he wanted to see a movie. Some romantic comedy. "

"I wish you could have come to D.C. last night."

She threw up her hands. "Impossible. I had work today. Anyway, it sounds like you brought in some fresh talent."

"We did. Philippe found them. Real players. They started us off with an old-fashioned strip show."

She giggled. "And then it became totally depraved."

"Wish you were there."

"David, I'm getting old."

"Don't be silly. If you're getting old then . . ."

"You're a man. A ridiculous old goat of a man, but nevertheless. What were they, twenty-two, twenty-three? I can't keep up with that."

This was true, about both of us. Claudette still made heads snap, and she still craved romantic adventure, but she was forty and couldn't rank with the uninhibited girls Philippe flew in from France. And, yes, I am a ridiculous old goat of a man, I knew it, but tonight was not the night I wanted to hear it. I was still troubled by the scarf girl's glib analysis, which didn't acknowledge the immensity of what was at stake. If the euro failed, there would be no simple reversion to national currencies. The northern economies would most likely retain the currency union while the southern nations drifted into crisis and indigence. The skinheads would take power in one country after another. They'd declare war on immigrants; also on ethnic and sexual minorities. Twenty years after the last division of Europe was erased, a new line would be drawn, a fault line that promised another century of brutality. My proposal was a problematic long shot, but this weekend, in the hours leading up to my meeting with the world's most powerful woman, I had to think of the plan and the man who devised it as something like heroic.

Claudette realized now that she had said the wrong thing and turned pensive. I let the moment grow, as a deterrent to further raillery along those lines, before I summoned our server. After watching Claudette suffer my disapproval, I gave the young woman a once-over. I offered Claudette a knowing look. She was just her type.

Claudette accepted my gesture as a pardon. When our meals arrived, I told her about Thursday night's proceedings in the capital, using some discretion so as not to disturb the sensibilities of the neighboring diners—though if they were actually listening they would have heard enough to be shocked, or intrigued, or aroused. I didn't mention Philippe's concerns or my appointment with Merkel. Yet she could see I was uneasy.

"Come on, David. Let's go to the hotel. You and me. A private party."

"I would like that."

"All right then. We can skip coffee."

Despite the hour, Claudette's eyes shone. She was lovely, men and women found her irresistible, and she was indisputably crazy about me. I waited several minutes before signaling for the bill.

"Should I ask the waitress to come up?"

"No! I want to be with *you*."

But once we left the restaurant, I turned away from the hotel. I insisted that we walk around the block, and then several blocks farther. Fetchingly unsteady in her heels, Claudette wrapped an arm around mine. We passed the closed scarf store, and the business card in the billfold resting against my chest pricked me like a thorn. Nearly as many people occupied the avenue as they did earlier in the evening. I inspected every one of them.

"How about her?" I whispered. "Nice breasts. Her? Him?"

She murmured appreciation. "Whoever you want, darling. I'm satisfied with a twosome tonight, really I am."

"I know." At that hour of the evening she would have been a comfort. When we moved the party to Thursday, I had thought I needed a full night's sleep before Saturday's transatlantic flight and my meeting with Merkel. Yet the thought of Merkel struck me now with great force, like a challenge. I asked Claudette, "How about Les Chiffres?"

"You're relentless!"

"Yes," I said, more grimly than I intended.

She considered. Les Chiffres was one of the most reliable and understated clubs in New York, with soft jazz, a hardwood dance floor, and subdued, flattering light. The cover was $300, keeping the crowd upscale and purposeful. "If you like. That's where we met that nice couple from Long Island last year."

Yes, I was relentless that evening, though the object of my resolve remained undefined. My mind seemed to be fixed on the possibility of complicated sexual partnering and a variety of sexual acts and positions, as if certain combinations and permutations of men and women could somehow be fitted into an algorithm or equation that would generate new, better equations, involving more bared, stroked organs, that would eventually, after several further sets of difficult computations, and more sex, describe the hidden lineaments of the universe. Meanwhile I wondered if we were being followed. I thought I saw on the street one of the men from the lobby.

Our taxi left us off in lower Manhattan at the metal door of a restaurant that seemed to have gone dark long ago. No signage was visible. I helped Claudette from the car and knocked twice. The door opened into a dimly lit space, occupied by a severe-looking woman in a man's tuxedo. Heavy velvet drapes loomed behind her. My Black Card parted them to reveal a convivial tableau of men and women in evening wear. As we entered the room, several turned in postures of expectancy and appraisal. Some trim, stylishly dressed couples shuffled around the postage-stamp dance floor. We ordered cognac at the bar.

Claudette left me while she cruised and a chanteuse lumbered through the Carla Bruni songbook. With no private rooms on-site, Les Chiffres was suitable only for introductions; even the bathrooms were patrolled. Claudette invited a man to dance and then, at the end of the song, his date. She led the girl, her hand low. Claudette's manner was easy and friendly, and she never pretended not to know why we had come. She was auditioning the couple for my benefit. They knew they were being auditioned and that I was watching. They looked my way several times. For the next song,

Claudette moved on to another man and woman, while I pondered the BlackBerry resting inside my jacket. I didn't know whether Geithner had returned my latest text. I needed one or two important commitments from Treasury. In a venue where strangers approached each other with the most intimate propositions, where women paraded in artful undress and the leer was accepted as a gracious compliment, looking at your phone was considered intolerably discourteous. I thought about which numbers I might tweak to make them more appealing to Merkel.

Claudette returned. I asked, "What do you think?"

"A slow night, I'm afraid."

I looked around. The banquettes were filled, several by guests in animated conversation that, for a moment, I longed to be part of. The women were pretty—too pretty to be DCRI, I thought, and then reconsidered. The intelligence agencies could have stepped up their game since the nineties, when I was last in government. Some of the men in the room looked as if they were limiting their drinks. I could tell that they were not only French but from the sector of society—striving lower-middle class, urban provincial—from which those agencies draw their personnel. I was conscious too that I might have been exaggerating my concerns. Philippe had heard vague rumors, not seen any evidence. The idea that I was being spied on in New York now seemed far-fetched.

"How about the redhead? She has legs like a racehorse."

"The guy's too hairy. Not my taste."

I gazed across the room at the redhead's stout, bearded date and thought of certain men for whom Claudette had raised her sweet derriere. Those partners had been no less hirsute than the date, who now looked away.

We spent another forty minutes or so at the bar, watching other couples make assignations. Anxiety visibly percolated through these exchanges as the would-be lovers courted rejection and then, having tentatively agreed in principle, attempted to negotiate a safe, convenient trysting place—some place like the Sofitel suite I had already booked, now sitting achingly empty. A group of six left together. Even though Claudette was by far the most attractive woman in the room, no one approached us.

At the same time I was easily the oldest man in the room and the only one in a business suit—a hand-tailored suit made of Italian linen, yes, but nevertheless these were the same clothes in which earlier that day, sweating and grunting, spitting and groaning, I had wrestled to the ground the unwieldy, oily numbers that underlay the disintegrating Greek economy. This was important work, important for Europe and the West. These were the labors that made possible, for instance, the existence of Les Chiffres, a venue for the exercise of sexual freedom within a society whose affluence made it tolerant of individual choice and secure enough for intimacy between strangers. Yet I felt foolish for coming, decrepit and needy, foolish for the entire day of women-hunting, and immensely fatigued. I leaned my head on Claudette's shoulder.

A town car took us back. I checked the phone once we were in the vehicle. Geithner had responded, finally, but the response was equivocal. I wouldn't be able to nail him down until after I spoke with Angela.

Claudette leaned close and kissed me tenderly, wrapping her hand around the inside of my leg. The gesture reminded me that we were returning to the Sofitel and I would be getting my reward: a piece that was in fact superior to any other that I had set eyes on that day (though the scarf girl was a close second). Yet my restlessness was only amplified. If some of Les Chiffres' guests were DCRI, pictures might have been taken, revealing my dishevelment. Perhaps the driver of the car was DCRI. He had arrived suspiciously soon after the hostess called. Claudette moved her hand up and I stiffened in the minute it took us to travel two city blocks. I had taken my Viagra in the Les Chiffres men's room, just as Claudette, similarly foresighted, was removing her panties in the women's.

We didn't speak as we slid into precoital anticipation. No surprises would present themselves tonight, we were too much like any other long-term couple that had shaped their lovemaking around the contours of their predilections, aversions, capabilities, and disabilities. Twenty-ninth Street. Thirtieth Street. Thirty-first. We knew exactly how events would unfold within three hundred seconds of arriving at Forty-fourth. Claudette had released her grip. With her eyes closed and her skirt pulled up, she was intently fingering herself. The driver might have been watching in the rear-view mirror, DCRI or not. She might have positioned herself so that he could watch.

Claudette was preparing for the moment we entered the suite. In the early, hopeful throbs of self-stimulation, she might have wagered that we wouldn't make it to the bed. We didn't. After our wordless elevator ascent, in which I sniffed and kissed her hand, the door's closing thud barely had time to echo off the neighboring, less libertine doors on the twenty-eighth floor. I threw her down to the carpet in the foyer. She landed on her shoulder, gasping. I dropped my pants.

This is how I prefer to have my women, and how they sometimes prefer it too, without the feints and hypocrisies of seduction, without the oversignificant looks and the lame jokes, in a sudden strike, a jump, a rage—a *coup de foudre*, a thunderbolt. This was how I had planned to take the red sheath and every other female I had encountered that day. Perhaps, because of the frustrations of the day, I may have used more force than was necessary. For a moment, before I fell on top of her, Claudette lay on the carpet stunned.

Later, when she emerged from the shower, she joked about her fall, though I could tell she was annoyed. I kissed the bruises tenderly. She left around four A.M. with the blue scarf tied around her neck, as would be recorded by the security cameras. The scarf suited her well, as if I had selected it with her neck in mind.

SEVEN

This brings us to Saturday, and then to my undoing. Thank you for bearing with me, Mariama—and since I'm not permitted to correspond with the actual Mariama, who I last saw fleeing my hotel suite in tears, I address the Mariama who hovers in the disturbed atmosphere above my laptop, the Mariama whose image occasionally flickers upon the interiors of my eyelids. In this account of my conduct, I have tried to be completely candid. I wonder if you're shocked, or whether you've seen men behaving much worse (in fact, it has been established that you have) or whether my power and wealth make me such an alien creature that my sexual deportment holds no more interest for you than, say, that of a mollusk at the bottom of the Atlantic.

Mariama, this account necessarily centers itself on my own preoccupations and actions, but I recognize that your days are no less dramatic than my own. Through press reports and my lawyers' research, I've studied the particulars of your difficult life (which I've made more difficult, though also different, with a new *aboutness*). I know that you're unmarried and that at the time of our encounter you lived with your teenage daughter in the Bronx district, in a tough *quartier* largely inhabited by other immigrants from West Africa. I know too that many of the flats in your building, and probably your flat too, are subsidized by a charitable agency that provides housing to people with HIV infection. I presume you're infected: your history demands it. And reaching these New York streets required struggle and guile, some of which would be uncovered by the legal process, to my lasting advantage.

On this bright spring morning, as you rode the subway into Manhattan, you must have dwelled on certain exigencies in your own life. Perhaps you were thinking of your daughter. I'm aware of the challenges: boys, crime, keeping up her school grades. I myself have four daughters, acquired over three marriages.

I never slept that morning. After Claudette departed, I sat at the desk in my underwear, studying the rescue plan and how it could be modified to account for projected German resistance. Although it was Saturday, European finance ministers with whom I'd consulted had gone to their offices to study the same figures without distraction, wondering the same thing. From time to time the assimilation of nitric oxide within my penis's corpora cavernosa led to an inflow of blood and I became hard again. In the last forty-eight hours I had slept less than two hours and swallowed three Viagras. I wished Claudette had stayed or that my wife was with me, or that they both were. I ordered breakfast and tried to revive my spirits by reviewing our early-morning lovemaking. Once she recovered from her fall, Claudette had been no less ferocious than I was. My right shoulder was raked by long, deep scratches. In the coming days, after my arrest and incarceration, I would watch the marks' gradual erasure with rising dismay. Within a week every sign of our caresses was gone.

My BlackBerry in-box was swimming with unread mail and texts. New data about Greece shortly arrived and demanded to be loaded into my calculations, threatening to upset the already listing rescue boat. I went down the queue. Most of the senders were from international lending institutions or European finance ministries. But several hours deep I recognized a name from another context, attached to a woman I had become acquainted with at a reception in the Petit Palais. She was a researcher in the UMP, Sarkozy's party. She had deflected my gallantries on several occasions, though not, I concluded, categorically. We had kept in touch.

It was a strange and alarming text. She wrote that the UMP had apparently obtained at least one e-mail that I had recently sent my wife through my BlackBerry. The researcher hadn't read the message herself but had overheard colleagues saying that it was related to what she tactfully called my "personal affairs."

This was, I realized, just what Philippe had warned me about. This was proof: I was under surveillance. Sarkozy was indeed employing the DCRI against me, a violation of law, principle, and common decency. My fantasies about the DCRI agents the night before were probably not fantasies at all. I was furious, in part because I had been shown to be naive. Although the president was my political opponent, I never really believed that he would go after me personally or compromise one of the nation's intelligence agencies. Conducting political espionage on American soil was especially reckless. Crazy, in fact.

Every e-mail and every text that I had written in the past week seemed to scroll before my eyes. Secret financial data. Communication with world leaders. Plans for the Thursday sex party. Endearments. Blandishments. Cajoleries. I fell into a trance as I realized all the forces that were being raised against me. There was only one person I could call in this situation: my wife. She was home in our apartment in Paris. We didn't need to exchange pleasantries.

"My phone's been tapped!" I cried. "Sarkozy's goons have at least one of our e-mails from last week."

"Oh, dear!" she said, her inflection sympathetically echoing my distress. I immediately felt better. She always knew how to pitch her responses to my travails, and also to my triumphs. She knew too about all my little vanities. She was my best friend, which makes her recent departure from my life, in a pall of mortification, the most tragic element of this entire affair. All right, you may not agree.

"Oh, baby," I said, sighing.

"Oh, honey," she murmured back. "Are you sure? Did they hack your account?"

"I don't know!" I paused to think about it. They would have had to penetrate the IMF's servers. "No. They must have gotten into the phone itself."

I instructed her to call my friend Victor, a public relations executive who handles certain political problems for me, including those having to do with security. He has his own contacts in French intelligence. Only a month before, in what I thought was an overabundance of caution, one of his men had installed an antibugging device in the BlackBerry. The only way it could have been disabled was by being physically removed.

"See if they'll come over tomorrow before I fly to Berlin. I want them to break the phone down to its circuits."

She said she would serve hors d'oeuvres. "By the way," she added, "which phone are you calling from?"

For the next twenty minutes after we abruptly ended our conversation, I stared at the treacherous BlackBerry. I tried to recall every instance in the last week in which the phone was removed from my possession. I was in my office most of that time, doing IMF business, with the phone on my desk or securely within my inside jacket pocket. I was usually without it only when I stepped into my private bathroom. At my Georgetown house, when my wife was with me, the device was placed in another room while we slept: she was annoyed when I woke to check my mail. But she hadn't been in Washington this week. I had left it on my night table. In the fresh, fragrant spring a screened window in the bedroom gazed upon our backyard garden and pool, plausibly accessible. The DCRI have good men for that type of operation.

Now, and not for the first time, I felt ambivalence and an actual revulsion toward my involvement in politics. I was reminded that this kind of aggressive, sordid behavior is a regular feature of political life, manifesting itself far in excess of and with greater virulence than a middle-aged technocrat's romantic adventuring. The men and women of power, whether they're Sarkozy or Merkel, Obama or Putin, are elementally no more than warlords, dedicated to their own survival and the domination of others. If they could murder their opponents, they would (and sometimes Putin does). Perhaps this is hardly a revelation for someone from Guinea, a country ruled by military dictators, Mariama, and I know it's a perspective shared by most people around the world. Criminality behind the facade of politics is a regular trope of popular culture. But I was squarely within the political process, I went into politics for love of country and a belief in humanity, and for me the abuse of power still provokes outrage.

I looked at my watch. I had a lunch date with my daughter Jeanne, who studies at Columbia and wished to introduce me to her fiancé. I was ambivalent about the lunch and the fiancé and couldn't remember where we were meeting, but the date had been made weeks before. After shaving, I rushed to take a quick shower.

The violated BlackBerry was still on my mind, as were my blunder in calling my wife from it, the Greek bailout (though we were not going to call it that), and my appointment with Angela, as were the indignities that the campaign was about to impose on me. I stopped soaping myself, paralyzed by anger. When I considered the limitations on my freedom of action, my temper began to rise. I knew I was being irrational, yet I felt now the weight of the world's many conspiracies. All my virtues—my intelligence, my idealism, and my passion—were being employed against me.

It was then that I became aware of my erection, my stupid, heavy, boring erection, rising blindly above the umbilicus, a growth between my legs, unbidden and unneeded. *Go away*, I thought. It was not the good, golden erection of youth, keenly animate, hypersensitive, throbbing, searching, yearning. No, no, it was a soulless, sixty-two-year-old, over-Viagraed dick. *Go away!* I touched it and there was no more feeling than if I had touched my elbow. I didn't think of masturbating. I was in a hurry, after all. I didn't yet realize how I might be delayed.

Now certain noises in the suite made themselves apparent to me. According to the later investigation, based on the keycard records, a room-service employee had arrived at 12:05 P.M. to take my breakfast dishes. He left. The shower was still beating down on my head. I shut it and began toweling off. Within a minute, at 12:06, the door to the suite opened again. When I heard that, I suddenly remembered the BlackBerry.

"Housekeeping!" you sang.

My first thought was that I had again foolishly left the phone unattended. After my indiscreet call to my wife, the DCRI knew that I would be having it inspected. They could enter the suite, find the phone, and take it.

"Hello!" you repeated. "It's Housekeeping!"

Hurriedly emerging from the bathroom, still dripping, I saw at once that the phone was unmolested. It was still on the night table. You stood nowhere near it. Again my fears were allayed, or shown to be misperceived, or overstated, or a chimera, or a figment.

You apologized. I hadn't even looked at you yet.

Your voice is lovely, Mariama, and I knew at once that you were an immigrant from French West Africa. As I've mentioned, I have some experience from development work in this region of the world, and it also provides me with profoundly erotic associations: the ribald cacophony of the markets; the indigenous art, stylized hermaphroditic figures carved from wood. My erection, which had only slightly subsided since I came out of the shower, now returned full force, full height, and full hardness, as big, I think, as it's ever been, after everything it had been through the past several days. My hand accidentally brushed against it, and the organ responded, finally, with a certain echoing murmur.

This was not the first time I've surprised a chambermaid; only rarely before have I done it without intention. This was probably not the first occasion on which you've been surprised. I'm sure most male travelers, even if they will deny it, have discovered the pleasing frisson that comes from presenting oneself naked to an unsuspecting hotel domestic.

Sometimes the thrill rises from the strangeness of the situation, in finding oneself completely unclothed, yet in this situation it's the *clothed* person who finds herself vulnerable. In her sleek or frilly costume, sexually suggestive regardless of the style, the maid always steps back, her eyes downcast, submissive and demure, and she apologizes for her intrusion. Her involuntary cry of astonishment often suggests something carnal. The surprise runs both ways. Until he steps from the hiding place, the hotel guest has no idea what the chambermaid will be like: large or petite, young or middle-aged, from the third world or from Eastern Europe. He will imbue his own apology with charm and mastery.

And this time there was the grandeur of my penis, which hovered in the atmosphere between us as sharp and full of intent as a spear. It was no longer stupid or boring. Empurpled, elevated, its delicate features in high relief, the phallus radiated heat and desire. The sight of a bared breast or another intimate female body part will sexually arouse almost any man, regardless of the woman to whom it belongs; in many situations it will stand as an invitation he can't resist. For a much smaller number of women, the presentation of an erection, especially one of noble proportions, serves as the same kind of incitement. Claudette is one of those women. My wife was once. Standing before you—the BlackBerry momentarily forgotten, proof yet again that the male reproductive organ may employ certain cogitative faculties and override others—I hoped to discover that you too belonged to that select sorority.

You and I alone know what happened next. I won't linger over the unfortunate episode, and when I return to it, the only purpose will be to clarify the record.

EIGHT

Every year nearly three million girls and young women in Africa and the Middle East undergo a procedure that removes sections of their external genitalia. This operation usually either severs the clitoral hood and the clitoris itself; severs the clitoris and the inner labia; or completely excises the clitoris and the inner and outer labia, followed by the fusion of the wound with a small hole left open to allow urination and the passage of menstrual blood. These measures are often performed by traditional practitioners, without the use of anesthesia—in some communities, the task falls to the local barber. According to Amnesty International, whose report has lain open on my desk for weeks, "broken glass, a tin lid, scissors, a razor blade, or some other cutting instrument" may be employed. The practice is perceived as a rite of passage into adulthood, further distinguishing women from men, especially in those communities where the clitoris is considered a vestigial "male part." The operation "purifies" a woman, preparing her for motherhood (though in the case of the third, most radical procedure, the "pharaonic circumcision," the suture has to be reopened at childbirth to allow passage from the birth canal). The practice's defenders call it vital to cultural identity, a heritage passed on from grandmother to mother to daughter. The principal purpose, however, is to minimize the potential for female sexual pleasure. In Guinea, according to the U.S. Department of State, 98.6 percent of all girls undergo the procedure.

I have several books laid out across my desk now. Numerous files are up on my laptop screen. This is what I've reconstructed from the public record and my lawyers' diligent investigation: Mariama Fofana, a native of a Fulani-speaking village in the Guinea highlands, was circumcised when she was seven, an operation for which she thanked neither her mother nor her grandmother, and which she refused to allow to be performed on her own daughter. Her principal motive in fleeing her homeland, an escape that demanded considerable courage, was to protect the girl from genital mutilation. Although she never experienced sexual pleasure herself and grew up in an environment in which female sexual pleasure was a dangerous contradiction of terms, Mariama took life-threatening risks and suffered hardship in recognition that sex was her daughter's birthright.

Other people's pursuit of sexual pleasure has brought Mariama nothing but misery and sickness. When she was twenty-two and already a mother, soldiers entered the village shop where she worked. They brought her and another woman to a local prison. The women were raped there. This may have been when Mariama acquired HIV. Another possibility is that she was infected by her husband. He would eventually die of AIDS. The actual HIV infection rate in Guinean adults is probably higher than the official figure of 1.7 percent. Retroviral drugs are unavailable beyond the country's main population centers.

Widowed, infected, illiterate, and impoverished, Mariama sought a more humane life for her child in the sanctuary of the West. The sanctuary is heavily guarded, of course; from the outside, it looks more like a fortress, with high-tech, weaponized ramparts. Every day thousands throw themselves at its walls in leaky boats that wash up on the beaches of the Mediterranean, or by trekking through the American desert, or by boarding airplanes with vague dreams and papers that will be contemptuously scrutinized—dreams and papers both. Even reaching the airport in Guinea's distant, lawless capital required heroic perseverance.

The documents Mariama presented to the steely-eyed officers at JFK were falsified, in the name of another woman. We don't know what she had to do, or sacrifice, to acquire them, or to what extent she trembled under the officers' examination. Once she reached the relative safety and experienced counsel of other West African immigrants in New York, she applied for political asylum. To improve her chances—and the asylum process did seem as cruel, arbitrary, and crooked as a casino game—she was advised to embellish her story. Desperate to remain in the States, she transformed herself and her late husband into opponents of the military regime. She invented another, even more brutal attack, this time a gang rape in retaliation for her political activities. She was beaten, she said, her two-year-old daughter was thrown to the ground, and their house was destroyed. Her husband was tortured and died as a political prisoner.

The prosecutor's discovery of these lies, which had nothing to do with what happened in the Sofitel, would impeach her credibility about what did happen in the Sofitel. These lies would save the middle-aged hotel guest accused of sexually assaulting her.

As the son of Jews who had their own cultural heritage to transmit, the guest was also circumcised. This is a much less consequential procedure for a man, with unknown harm and uncertain benefits. The foreskin seems to serve no biological purpose. The effects of circumcision on the sexual experience have not been conclusively determined by medical science, despite decades of ingenious experimentation.

Even now the man gazes at his circumcised penis, tender in its repose, brutal in its rampancy, and marvels at the organ's physiognomy. Some proponents of male circumcision claim that the removal of the foreskin heightens sexual pleasure because the procedure exposes more fine-touch neuroreceptors to the object of its pursuit. That may be correct, but the foreskin possesses neuroreceptors too. The intact foreskin, with its distinctive anatomy and points of sensitivity, may attain another dimension of sexual pleasure that the circumcised can't imagine, and the loss of which can't be imagined by the uncircumcised. The man has often wished there were some way to find out.

For the millions of women who can't experience clitoral stimulation, this emphasis on sexual pleasure may seem perverse, but the impulse and opportunity to make love for one's own amusement is a defining quality of civilization. Education launches young people into an adulthood free of parental control. When they move to urban places, their choices about where to work, live, and make purchases confirm their independence. Civilizing manners and protective legal structures allow women to join the company of men safely. Then they may choose whom to love. They employ contraceptive technology to separate their sex lives from their roles as mothers. Mutually gratifying intimacy becomes a respected value. In a world whose history has been dominated by communal identity, whether familial, tribal, or national, the right to sexual pleasure defiantly affirms the primacy of the individual. When the International Monetary Fund lends a troubled nation money for economic development, the institution is clearing the way to a freer, more joyous, and more loving sex life for its people.

The hotel guest's was probably the first circumcised penis that Mariama ever saw. She must have been horrified. Whatever revulsion she may have felt toward his mutilated organ could only have intensified when he tried to put it in her mouth.

NINE

Mariama, I've already suggested enough about our encounter to have me indicted, extradited from France, convicted, put away for years in a New York prison, and, on the civil side, bankrupted along with my ex-wife, whose lawyers have not yet succeeded in fully shielding her assets.

Yet the full narrative, the whole truth, continues to elude me. I rise from my desk and pace across the room.

I gaze onto the Montparnasse street's rain-blackened cobblestones. I return to the laptop screen. I play with words and then with Word, changing fonts as if I may discover the single correct typeface designed for reviled ex-politicians charged with two counts of criminal sexual acts, one count of attempted rape, two counts of sexual abuse, one count of unlawful imprisonment, and one count of forcible touching. I've tried altering the color of the type as well.

In my frustration and impatience I've now transferred this commentary out of Word to another program, the one for which I compose and send e-mails. I've pasted everything I've written so far under the address and subject lines. It feels much more like a confession this way. You probably don't have an e-mail address, but your lawyer does. I've copied it from one of his professional communications to my lawyers. I've typed his address in the *To:* line, to see what it looks like. It looks hazardous.

Now, as I pause to consider the rest of the day of our encounter, I play with the touch pad below my keyboard, gliding the cursor across the screen. The arrow inevitably approaches the pink SEND button. It circles around the edge of the device and gently caresses it. When the arrow passes over the rectangle, the button reddens as if it were a nipple. I pull the arrow away and then, my index finger still stroking the touch pad, I return. The color turns again. I caution my index finger not to double-tap.

TEN

I checked out of the hotel at 12:28, according to the security cameras in the lobby, twenty-two minutes after you entered my suite. It has now been established that I left without my BlackBerry. Unforgivably late for lunch with my daughter, I hailed a taxi to transport me the seven blocks to the restaurant.

This letter is an account of my many foolish, perverse actions that weekend; almost chief among them was taking a taxi to travel seven Manhattan blocks. No sooner had I entered the cab then we were immobilized in suddenly congealed traffic. The crosstown traffic was stuck too, blocking the next several intersections. We waited through two cycles of stoplights, and then my taxi, pretending to see daylight, lurched forward and stopped again.

In a day of my life whose many dismal moments were recorded by keycards, security cameras, and cell phone logs, the only passage of time was now marked by the taximeter. An uptick of forty cents announced the expiration of one minute and then the next. Horns sounded. Men shouted.

The traffic shuddered in its pent-up fury. Other cars and trucks crowded into our lane, every vehicle looking for an opening or some kind of advantage. Trapped in the backseat like a hamster in a glass tank, I looked out and around frantically. The air shimmered from exhaust and radiator heat. Sarkozy and the press were in the cars on either side of us. They flashed their cameras and iPhones. I peered through the windshield. Angela Merkel was at the wheel of the Mercedes ahead, tapping the brake more heavily than was necessary. On the sidewalk, pedestrians passed the stalled cars and vanished below the horizon.

I wondered if I should throw the driver a twenty, leave the cab, and walk the rest of the way. But what if traffic should start moving? I was already more than thirty minutes late. After acting so decisively in the hotel room, I was now unable to move from the edge of my seat. I feared that after I walked a block I'd watch the taxi pass. But if I remained in the cab it seemed that I would never reach the restaurant at all. The issue weighed on me as heavily as a complicated politico-economic problem, or as vexingly as a delicate moral conundrum.

"Fucking Greeks," the cabdriver said. I concurred and was about to add that the European Central Bank should have reviewed Athens' public-sector contracts two years ago, when I realized that Sixth Avenue was blocked ahead by a street fair. Every stall offered a sizzling hunk of meat pressed on a spit.

The driver abruptly turned left on Forty-seventh Street, detouring to Eighth Avenue to resume our crawl uptown. The actual distance to my destination was now greater than it had been at the hotel. It was already too late to get out.

By the time I made it to the restaurant, my daughter was glowering. I apologized, fully earnest. About to reach inside my jacket pocket for the phone, I said I could stay only briefly, before catching a cab to JFK. "In that case," Jeanne replied, as sternly as my first wife, her mother, would have, "don't even think of checking your mail."

The fiancé made no impression, and I couldn't tell you which species of animal provided my lunch or what was the subject of my conversation with the two young people, or whether I thought they were truly in love. (They soon disengaged, unable to withstand the corollary gusts and squalls that blew around the tornado of my arrest.) While the boyfriend explained his studies, I reflected on my encounter with you, those moments of physical contact. I had been a brute, of course, and I already deeply regretted it. Looking down at you on the other side of my engorged penis, I had seen desperate fear in your eyes, and still I forced myself on you. Philippe was correct, I had to stop this behavior. I was out of control. And then, in a moment of grave error, I picked up the cash (yes, *that* cash, that only you and I know about).

I paid for lunch, kissed both of them on their cheeks, and hailed another taxi to the airport. Before the vehicle had traveled a block, I finally went to check my phone. But the jacket pocket was empty. The shock was nearly as great as if I had found the sleeve empty too.

I took a spare phone from my briefcase, called the lost phone, and received a message saying that it was out of service. I knew of course that it was most likely left at the hotel. I used it while you were in the room, to return a call from my daughter. Then what did I do with it? Did I lay it on the unmade bed? It probably fell and bounced out of sight under the bed.

No, no, no, you idiot. You left it on the windowsill!

I was already late for my plane. If I returned, I would risk missing the flight. Now a full hour passed in congestion and construction detours. The driver impulsively switched to blocked lanes, allowed other cars to cut in front, and missed the turnoff to the Van Wyck—making me wonder if he too were DCRI. I was faced with a serious dilemma. It was imperative to have the phone returned. The device had access to the IMF's classified technical data, and most important, the evidence of tampering was nestled among its chips. Made public, this evidence would be my best defense against my opponents, and possibly, if the bugging mechanism could be traced all the way to the Élysée Palace, it would bring down Sarkozy. I'd walk into the presidency unimpeded.

At the same time, Mariama, yes, I was aware that I had behaved badly at the hotel. I thought I would have to reserve a room somewhere else the next time I came to New York. I may even have begun to dimly sense that some sort of legal cloud might be suspended over my last twenty minutes in the suite. Someone could have heard us. You could have told somebody. My head spun as I tried to balance the recollection of my offense, the consequences of losing the phone, and the political benefits that would accrue from recovering it. I understood the good practical reasons for not trying to contact the hotel that afternoon.

But I needed the phone and my concerns were only abstractions, the result, I presumed, of overthinking the situation. I had taken chambermaids before and never had a problem. With that last happy thought in mind, I called the hotel, identified myself, and explained about the lost device. I realize now that I was not asked to repeat my name, not once, nor asked where I might have left the phone. Instead, I was directly transferred to what I was told was Lost and Found. The gentlemen there said he would look for the BlackBerry and asked for my current location and the number of the phone that I was calling from.

As I know now, the employee, surprised by my call, was being coached by a fast-thinking New York City detective. While I was having my forgettable lunch, you had cried out to your floor supervisor that you had been assaulted. With great difficulty, over a full hour, your co-workers persuaded you to put your trust in the law—something which, in the course of your life, had never once recognized your humanity. They called 911 for you. But even before the police arrived, certain other employees had entered the presidential suite and searched it, according to the keycard records. They evidently discovered the BlackBerry—and that was the stroke of pure luck that they would be seen celebrating on the hotel security cameras a few minutes later. The men did not reveal the phone's recovery to the police. They still deny it, and they say they can't recall why they were high-fiving and embracing each other. They also deny any connection to French intelligence.

My own detectives have investigated the possibility that you were involved in a conspiracy to retrieve the BlackBerry on the DCRI's behalf, either with or without your knowledge. They have studied every possible scenario; not a single one is as plausible as the simplest, in which, in the heat of the moment and the rush to check out, I left the device behind. It wasn't the first time I had misplaced a phone.

As I reached the airport, another individual, saying he was from the hotel's front desk, called to say he had the phone in his possession. My suspicions were not raised. He said he'd deliver it to me at the airport and asked for my flight information. Please hurry, I said, unaware that I was designing my own trap, constructing my cell at Rikers Island bar by bar. He assured me that the plane would be held if necessary. Given my official status, of course it would be held, I thought. I decided that $100 would be a sufficient gratuity.

Believing that the BlackBerry would soon be returned, I looked forward to a nap, if only for a few hours. The past several days had been difficult, and I was still facing Merkel on Sunday. We boarded the aircraft. I took my seat in first class and noted with satisfaction that the traveler in the window seat was a dark-haired European woman in her thirties, her lipstick and eyeliner sharply applied. She didn't smile, but that could have been corrected.

When the door to the plane was finally reopened to admit the man from the hotel, the sound of the air rushing in was as soft as a kiss.

ELEVEN

Our common history began with a kiss, though you can't possibly recall the kiss, not with everything else that happened in the next twenty minutes. I've probably forgotten elements of the encounter too, though what I do remember is painful enough and sufficiently criminal. As you may have observed, I've hesitated before directly addressing our time together. The public record is silent about these minutes, except for the statement you made to the police, which comprises several misrepresentations that serve to construct a less complicated, less morally ambiguous narrative of the affair. The true narrative will hardly acquit me, but to comprehend my actions and yours, I will have to review the events fully, with all their intricacies and qualifications intact.

When I emerged from the shower, you were crossing the doorway into the bedroom. You stopped suddenly, once my motion was visible from the corner of your eye. In accordance with the script, with which I was already familiar from similar encounters in Buenos Aries, Moscow, and Phnom Penh, you looked away and recoiled as if at the edge of a subway platform from a rushing train. You cried, "I'm sorry, sir! I didn't know you were here!"

If I were following the same script I would simply have covered myself, apologized in turn, and left you an extra twenty when I checked out. But in my excited anticipation, and perhaps concurrently experiencing several other confused mental states, I had forgotten the towel. In fact I was still wet, dripping on the bedroom carpet. Despite the resolve with which I was about to act, my thoughts were multiform and quicksilverish. In the moments before I crossed the space between us, I recalled again all the forces that were arrayed against me, including the stubborn Angela Merkel. Tomorrow she would declare that she could not ask German taxpayers to subsidize Greek indolence, which was pure political boilerplate, when what was needed was to steady the markets—including the German stock exchange, which had been declining all week. Now forex options were taking a hit. I wondered if a mechanism that would narrow the eurozone's interest-rate spread would make the plan more acceptable. It's possible that when I saw you before me, Mariama, full-bodied, round-eyed, unaffectedly styled, and unrevealing, I mistook you for the German chancellor herself.

Even with my erection waving in front of you like a baton, our first contact was with my lips. You shrieked and turned away. My mouth came down on the back of your head. Your hair was surprisingly soft, as if it had just been washed. I squeezed your breasts, each of them entombed within a matronly brassiere, and I slid around you into the hallway to shut the door to the suite. I returned.

"My darling, there's nothing to be sorry for," I said, taking you by the shoulders and pushing you toward the unmade bed, still sweetly ripe, I think, with Claudette's scent.

"Please, mister!" you said, struggling in my grip.

"Just listen to me."

I gave you a smile and my full warm-eyed regard. Later news reports suggested that you're an unattractive woman, stressing your excess weight, your troubled complexion, and your unfashionably flat hair. The idea was that you were a person unworthy of sexual attention, which I would publicly dispute if only I had the chance. No, Mariama, don't pay heed to the belittling passersby. Physical features and style are superficial elements of romantic appeal. Men and women bear within something deeper, more personal, more occult, and more wonderful: indestructible beacons of compassion and animal need. That is the source of our beauty. Every person is worthy of sexual attention. Our fundamental human dignity demands it.

"I will come back later."

I said, "Please, dear, give me the opportunity to persuade you."

"This is wrong," you said firmly.

"How would you know if you don't allow me to present the data?"

I gently stroked my erection, just inches away from your face. From this gesture came an upwelling of sweet sensation.

"I can't afford to lose my job!" you cried, and you bolted for the door. I grabbed you by the shoulders and pulled you back to the bed. You resisted, of course, but not with all the muscle that you could have applied. You're several inches taller than me, and perhaps thirty pounds heavier. You recognized that I was a guest, staying in a suite reserved for the rich and powerful. You feared that you might hurt me, even minimally—and then you would certainly lose your job, your single toehold on a notch cut into the sheer slate walls of the New York canyons, the only possible shelter for you and your daughter in a hostile world. I was aware of these considerations, but I also judged the deficit of force to be a kind of partial acquiescence, or at least an opening for negotiation.

"Ha-ha," I said, and added, with I suppose telling insouciance, "I'm more likely to lose mine!"

I shoved you down against the edge of the bed and brought my penis in front of your face. You whipped your head away. My erection brushed your cheek several times. I couldn't get it between your lips, though.

Then you pushed hard against my lower chest, slamming me against the wall, and the edge of the dresser caught my side. Oh, baby. The pain was brief but enormous. My erection was not diminished. The pain may have keyed it up further, reminding every nerve of the life-giving, life-defining richness of physical sensibility.

You paused for a moment, frightened by the violence of your reflex.

"My supervisor's in the hall! She'll hear us!"

This was a bluff, but now my BlackBerry rang. We both turned toward the device, which lay on the night table beside us, as if someone else had indeed come into the room, and we waited for it to finish.

I couldn't help myself. I looked at the phone. Could it be Geithner? No, the call had been from my daughter. It was already past noon; 12:13, according to the BlackBerry records.

I turned away from the phone. "I'll pay you!"

"I'm not like that!"

"A thousand dollars," I proposed. You've never revealed this to the prosecutors. You may never have even revealed it to your lawyers. I said, "Two thousand dollars!"

You took off down the windowed hall toward the bathroom, hoping to lock yourself inside. As you know, however, it's a large suite, large enough for a small reception, and sometimes a sex party, and I caught you before you could reach it. I pinned you against the wall and groped under your uniform dress while you cried, "No, no, no!" and tried to push me away. I caught the elastic band and pulled down your pantyhose. You can imagine my surprise when I found another pair beneath it.

I had never encountered a second pair of pantyhose before and would never have expected one on a warm spring morning in New York. The encasement of your sex in so much nylon convinced me only that it was a greater prize than I had suspected and perhaps, I thought, in the madness of the moment, greater than any sex I had ever known. I reached under the second pair, almost expecting a third, and at last found that hoarded, already heavily contested treasure, your vagina.

You shrieked again and knocked me away, but I pushed you down to the floor, against the wall. You leaned back, threatening to kick me with your heavy, black uniform shoes.

"Wait a minute," I said, panting.

"Please, mister!"

I stood over you menacingly, still with the phone in my hand and my dick in your face. I thumbed the return-call button. The time was 12:15.

My daughter picked up immediately. "Where are you!"

"Delayed at the hotel, honey. I'm sorry, where's the restaurant again?"

You moved as if to escape, but I came in closer to your head, my legs on either side of you, my torso blocking you from rising or rolling away. Unsmiling now, I locked my eyes with yours, communicating my resolve.

"Dad! McCormick & Schmick's, on Fifty-second Street! Between Sixth and Seventh!"

I tried to stifle my groan. With thousands of sophisticated, distinctive places to eat in New York, she picked a chain restaurant.

"We went through this already," she complained. "You wanted something near the hotel. Remember?"

"Right," I grunted.

"The reservation was for noon."

"I thought twelve thirty," I lied.

"Noon!"

I stroked my cock again, to assure that it was hard, an unnecessary precaution. My full testicles dangled before your eyes. I leaned one of my knees into your shoulder, keeping you there. It must have hurt, and an MRI would later show a ligament tear.

"Order some appetizers, I had some business. I'm seeing Angela Merkel."

"I know."

"I'll be there in a minute." I disconnected.

If we had gone to trial, the thirty-six seconds occupied by the phone call would have been decisive in my defense. My lawyers would have argued persuasively (they are high-priced lawyers) that you could have pushed your way past me and fled the suite. They would have called expert witnesses; they might have produced a reenactment. My defense team would have told the jury that you remained to consider my offer. Shrewdly anticipating this argument, you lied to the police when you were interviewed. You told them that my assault was completed and that you had left the room before I received any phone calls. That would have been within seven minutes of entering the hotel suite. Because the keycards don't record exits, there's no evidence that you left when you say you did.

"Two thousand dollars," I repeated, reaching around a curtain to put the phone on the windowsill. The drapery immediately fell back to conceal it.

"Noooo," you keened, your eyes gone glassy.

"Do it." I grabbed you by your hair and pulled your head back. I made a mental note to retrieve the phone later. "Do it! I'll pay you."

This time I succeeded in forcing my penis into your mouth, but for no more than twenty seconds. In the state of excitement heightened by our scuffle, all I needed were those moments of heat and wetness transmitted by your mouth's mucous membrane. Oh, darling, I can summon to memory every ridge and contour of your tongue and palate. My ejaculation was hardly powerful or voluminous, or even a pleasant physical sensation, but it produced a quickening of my spirit, a release against constraint, and a perception of control over events that were absent from my every other sexual climax of the past two days.

When I was done, I withdrew my still swollen organ, spooling out a delicate spider's filament of semen between the glans and your lips, our last contact, and you began to spit. Some of the semen spilled out around the sides of your mouth. The tears ran down your cheeks unevenly.

You stared past the hand I extended to help you up. I gave you another moment. Then I walked into the bedroom to the dresser and opened my wallet. Before I could finish counting out the hundreds, you ran from the suite, your steps pounding hard on the carpet. I left the money on the night table.

Mariama, you must recognize that I was fully conscious, even at that moment, of the magnitude of my misconduct. Regardless of the defense my lawyers would have successfully advanced, I knew that you never consented to fellate me. A man with four daughters, a man who loves women—desperately of course, and frequently to his disadvantage—I tasted remorse as bitter as the probably immotile ejaculate that you were still trying to clear from your mouth. The depths of my depravity were now fully plumbed, I told myself. Hurrying to dress and brush my teeth, I swore that I would never do anything like this again, at least not while I was running for office.

I took my bag, including yesterday's well-used underwear and shirt, but forgot to retrieve the hidden BlackBerry from the windowsill. The money still lay on the night table, a stack of $100 bills fluttering in the air-conditioned breeze. My mind raced from the thrill of our encounter to the urgency of my lunch date. I wondered if I should leave the bills. You were emphatic in your refusal to take them. If the $2,000 simply remained there, it would serve as evidence of my wrongdoing, or at least raise questions. Just as I left the suite, I scooped up the cash and returned it to my wallet.

A mistake, of course. I wasn't thinking clearly. I had already turned my mind to the question of how to reach McCormick & Schmick's. Without thinking it through, I had taken your refusal of payment at face value. I descended to the lobby, where security cameras showed me exiting the elevator at 12:27:06.

Meanwhile, the hotel's keycard records show that you returned to the presidential suite at 12:26, seconds after I left. You had apparently been hiding down the hallway, waiting. Another minute passed before you exited the suite and reported the assault to your supervisor, tearfully, just as she arrived on the twenty-eighth floor. You were still upset and still trying to expectorate. The prosecutors would find it odd, even inexplicable, and then suspicious that you went back to the suite with the taste of my semen in your mouth.

What happened in that minute?

I know what happened in that minute. You were thinking that perhaps you wouldn't report the assault, in your innocence fearing that you would be fired for your improper relations with an important guest and your forcible resistance against him. You may have thought that your immigration status and your daughter's would be jeopardized. Perhaps you would lose access to the retroviral drugs that keep you alive. You then entertained second thoughts about my offer. Two thousand dollars is a lot of money for someone in your position. You had already earned it, whether willingly or not. If you were going to stay silent, you thought, you might as well take the cash.

But on entering the bedroom you discovered that the money was gone. All that you found in the presidential suite was an unmade bed, against the edge of which I had pushed you, the hallway down which you had been pursued, the place where I had torn your pantyhose and grabbed at your vagina—the red-hot center of your misfortune—and the wall at the end of the hallway in which you had been forced to perform oral sex. Gobs combining my semen and your saliva glistened at the tips of the carpet threads. You stared at the night table, surprised at your conviction that the money would be there. Of course it wasn't there. In that moment all the things that had transpired in your life, all the crimes that had been committed against you, were being made evident—the circumcision, the rapes, the infection, and countless other sorrows that come from being a woman in the third world, plus my sexual assault. Now you were being mocked by the naked night table. On this day you had not only been assaulted, you had been robbed. This was a nightmare, this was a catastrophe, this was something that you thought would never happen to you in America. Of course you were upset. In that same minute your floor supervisor arrived. It would have been impossible not to cry out.

So Angela Merkel kept her Sunday free after all. I imagine she weeded her garden. On Monday the markets declined sharply, and by the end of the week they had crashed across the board. Standard & Poor's cut Italy's credit rating. Portuguese bonds fell to junk status. The European debt crisis continues to eat away at the livelihoods and well-being of millions of people on the Continent and around the world. Slowly, painfully, sullenly, the Germans have agreed to half measures considerably less effective than the plan I would have advocated if I had not been locked in a cell on Rikers Island. Their bailout will cost far more than mine would have, especially if it had been executed at once—*suddenly*—before the brutal damage was done. Official unemployment in Greece is now 25 percent. Governments have fallen from Dublin to Prague. Many decades will pass before we see a restoration of Europe's confidence in its democratic institutions, if they even survive. Fractious and impoverished, and on courses that are unsustainable in every direction, the rest of the world will suffer from our loss of leadership. Europe may be a ridiculous old goat of a continent, but it is also the repository of the world's most vital humanist values.

Perhaps not every detail in my account is accurate. If, in fact, it were possible to contact each other, you might jog my memory or clarify certain aspects of your actions and responses. You would then remind me of the personal consequences suffered by you and your loved ones. I would be obliged to more fully acknowledge them. I might then speak of my wife's devastating grief. We would exchange confidences. Perhaps then I would devise the correct words in which to begin to formulate an apology. Until we correspond, I can reconstruct the narrative of our encounter only imperfectly, incompletely, and inconclusively, unable to find my way back to the right and just. The SEND button still hovers at the top of my screen. It throbs beneath the touch of the arrow. Its heat is transmitted through the touch pad. I could double-tap it now. The e-mail would strike your lawyer like a thunderbolt.

Part II
Factitious Airs

THE MOMENT THEY WERE WAITING FOR

His crime was unspeakably foul; his guilt was unquestionably manifest; he offered no tremor of remorse. In a trial that conformed to every legal norm, Lester Ganz was convicted and sentenced to die.

The murderer had glared defiance at the judge and jury. He turned to stare down the courtroom spectators, one by one. Even his lawyer, a future suicide, cringed from Ganz's regard. They all feared Ganz as a creature dredged up from the underworld, vile and malignant. Before the sentence was issued, the judge reminded the courtroom of the murder's heartbreaking particulars; Ganz snickered. Yet once the judge pronounced the punishment, Ganz's bravado was shattered. The killer sharply sucked in his breath and left his mouth gaping. He seemed surprised, especially on hearing the appointed date of his execution. The young prison warden, in the second row of spectators, took note of Ganz's response. He would recall it later, in the grotesque aftermath.

The execution was set to take place within two months, and the city was inflamed with anticipation. Even those citizens who claimed indifference counted down the weeks. Every day of the final week seemed to exist only in relation to the designated day, a Tuesday. The warden observed that a mysterious process had taken place since Ganz's sentence was read. The murderer had been severed from the murder; the public imagination had surged forward to the death chamber, carrying with it an undertow of sympathy. The newspapers lingered over the procedure by which the lethal injection would be administered. Readers shivered as if their own arms lay within the needle's predetermined course.

The warden, who would be presiding over his first execution, had previously entertained no qualms about capital punishment. Now he steeled himself by recalling the viciousness of the murder. He studied the coroner's report. He reminded himself that he was no more than an instrument of the criminal justice system.

Ganz's imagination worked no less vividly than the public's. Alone in his cell, he too counted the days, amazed as each sparked out. He had never loved life and had seemed to seek annihilation since his first stick-up, but now he was consumed by the concrete image of himself being strapped to the gurney at a known, fixed moment in the future. Every intervening second represented a quantifiable fraction of his existence. Ganz lay on his bunk, his face drained of color, his eyes glassy. As the final moments of his life passed like sand uselessly through his fingers, Ganz could hardly complete a thought. He became powerfully aware of what other men knew only dimly or imperfectly or tried to forget: that their motion through time was relentless.

The warden accompanied prison guards and other visitors to the cell, to ensure that every formality was observed. As the execution approached, Ganz showed little awareness of his surroundings. When he did take notice, it was only to scrutinize the warden: his pressed suit, his unlined face, his clear eyes, his future. And then Ganz would close his eyes, drawing within himself as he had been doing for weeks now, in communication, perhaps, with whatever spirits had led him to evil in the first place. The warden wished that the hours would somehow hurry themselves to the appointed date.

The date arrived. The execution was scheduled for nine in the morning, suggesting that it was merely an ordinary day's first item of business, but the prison was lit all night, humming in preparation. A last meal was brought and refused; the transaction was given grave ceremony by the draped food cart, the polished hoods over the serving dishes, and the curious, lingering deliveryman, who had won the task from his co-workers in an impromptu raffle. The prisoner was taken from his cell. The warden expected that tension would have further dulled Ganz's senses; this morning, however, he was alert and still vital and dangerous, though bound in the grip of large, armed men. He struggled against each inevitable step. At the entrance to the death chamber, where lawyers and officials were gathered around the apparatus, he emitted a low growl. Facing the last men he would ever see, he fixed his eyes on the warden's, holding them in an implacable embrace. At that moment the warden believed that Ganz knew him like no other human being. The warden looked away, aware of his own cowardice.

Ganz was fastened to the gurney, whose straps and other constraints he had already imagined completely. Just as the needle was inserted, he swore—it was an oath of nearly heroic coarseness—and he muttered something additional under his breath. The warden, standing at his side, thought he heard a burst of tortured syllables from some foreign, malevolent language. The speech carried the urgency of a promise. And then, finally, exactly as the judge had foretold, Lester Ganz was dead.

The body was promptly taken away. The officials who had attended the execution took leave of one another with somber handshakes and regret that even these gestures excessively honored that morning's nastiness. At the same time they felt swindled, for the murderer's punishment was concluded and couldn't compensate for his crime's enduring wrong. The newspapers published extras that seemed anticlimactic and sold poorly. The warden went to his office fatigued from sleeplessness and stress. Outside his window the overcast sky was oddly lit, taking on a yellowish tint, and gusts swirled rubbish in the exercise yard. The hushed city turned slowly through the hours. Men and women went about their business with their heads down, eager for this day to pass into oblivion.

The horrific new era dawned the following day, a Wednesday. With the execution finally behind him, it should have been an uneventful morning, but the warden rose from sleep murmuring certain words and numbers: a month, a day of the month, and a year sometime in the future. He didn't recall a relevant dream, and the memory of it remained intact, unlike the memory of a dream. He shaved and dressed, puzzled. The year was so remote that it suggested a fantastically new world, but his dream had not been accompanied by a vision of scientific marvels or social revolution. Although he didn't speak of it with anyone, that day he several times stopped what he was doing, looked up from his desk, and silently mouthed the date, to make sure that he still remembered it.

Others did the same. By the end of the week it was known that everyone in the city had awakened that morning with some future date on his or her lips. Inevitably they compared the dates; when patients in the city hospital ward revealed that theirs were proximate and then died on them, the city's residents realized that they had been granted knowledge of their own death dates.

Skepticism was voiced about the phenomenon, with the Mayor scorning mass hallucination and hysteria, and no one except the warden connected it immediately to the execution of Lester Ganz. Despite the official ridicule, husbands, wives, lovers, and friends rushed to announce their dates and then stepped away to consider what each other's meant for them personally. In the next few weeks, as the mortally ill continued to pass away on schedule and healthy citizens perished in unforeseen but punctual accidents, the city came to understand that it had been set apart from the rest of humanity. It had been cursed. Once the association with Ganz was made, his body was disinterred and incinerated in an ad hoc midnight ceremony attended by clergy, but this had no practical effect.

The warden's own death was put off well into the next century, a distant point in time, it seemed, when he would be ninety-three. His fiancée revealed that hers would come soon, just four years hence—in childbirth? she wondered, having always been apprehensive about giving birth. She broke off the engagement and forswore having children. Avoiding a bereavement that would complicate the long decades to follow, the warden was secretly relieved. Four years later the woman died of an illness unrelated to pregnancy; it was an affliction, in fact, popularly associated with spinsterhood.

The city's inhabitants had known they were mortal, but awareness of the dates their mortality would take effect enshrouded them in perpetual mourning for themselves and their loved ones. Even those who had been promised extended life spans considered their grasp on existence only tenuous. A few individuals responded with the determination to occupy their meticulously allotted years with purposeful activity, making lists of what they expected to accomplish and when. Like other people, however, they were eventually overcome by lassitude, as if the moment they had been waiting for were already at hand. In their hours of greatest pleasure, sharing a good meal with friends or playing catch with their children on a hazy summer morning, no one could escape the thought: *this too shall pass*.

Attempts to thwart Ganz's curse always failed. Those who sought to take their own lives ahead of time survived their razor blades and nooses and their dives off cliffs, only to be badly hurt and to succumb to their injuries on the correct date anyway. Even when a person believed he had devised foolproof means of premature self-destruction, he was somehow waylaid or injured before it could be accomplished. Suicide was more successfully pursued by individuals who waited until their appointed date and accomplished it early in the day, consoled that they had at least chosen their own means of departure. They were seen to have kept their composure. Others had not, their mental health undermined by the accelerating approach of their death dates until they reached those days in a fury of suicidal madness; the foreknowledge itself was the cause of death. In truth, it was impossible to tell these two classes of suicides apart. The awareness of one's death date superseded every other cause of neurosis and psychosis.

So that a pall would not be cast over their classrooms (for Ganz's curse had not spared the city's children), schoolteachers invented a calendar composed of 10-day weeks and 45- and 46-day renamed months and 730-day renumbered years. The city eventually adopted the calendar for its public business, and newspapers jettisoned conventional Gregorian dates from their front pages. None of this erased Ganz's malediction. The rest of the world continued to call the days, months, and years by their fatal names, and the city could not wall off its knowledge of them; no individual could forget the simple fact of his death date. Some residents fled in the desperate hope that absence from the city would invalidate the prophecies. Fate caught up with them in Marseilles barrooms, Rangoon infirmaries, and Argentine train wrecks.

In the city, birthdays were hardly observed, but the anniversary of one's future death—which elsewhere passed every year unremarked—became the occasion for lavish social events. Prayers and elegies gave the affairs a certain gravity, yet congratulations were made and presents were exchanged. One customary gift was a watch whose hands rotated counterclockwise. The usual humorous birthday comments about aging and the accumulation of years—a bit derisive, a bit nervous—were replaced by similarly unfunny, self-conscious comments about their dwindling. The honorees would smile blankly and attend the festivities with an air of distraction, aware that they were commemorating their prospective absence. The following morning they would wake surprised by life, unsure of their surroundings, imagining the odor of sulfur in their nostrils.

People planned their lives according to their deaths. Men and women searched for mates with congruent life expectancies, and one occasionally found another who would perish on the same date—together, they assumed romantically. Individuals were now able to more rigorously organize their finances, their retirements, and the purchase of goods whose expiration could be foreseen, such as refrigerators and bananas. Sinners gave themselves just enough time to repent and alter course. No one died without the last-minute opportunity to confess their love (though many, sadly, did not).

The city became an unruly place as its inhabitants calculated and recalculated their choices within their precisely known quantities of remaining life.

Their predictions, which were as accurate as if their deaths had already happened in the known past, raised doubts about the reality of time as a physical phenomenon. Time was now reckoned as elusive and illusory, something experienced psychologically, measurable but closed to empirical investigation. Some people believed that every event in the city's history took place at once, in a single, eternal, unchanging moment, which was only *perceived* as plural. The ball was pitched in the same *now* as the one in which the ball was hit. Two lovers' first kiss occurred simultaneously with their last betrayal. In this blighted quadrant of the universe, residents were guaranteed a static immortality.

Nevertheless, not a day went by in which someone did not try to defy the prophecy that had issued from his own lips. Men and women in good health arrived at their death dates with the determination not to leave their homes. Occupying their last days in their living-room easy chairs, they were killed by strokes, house fires, food poisoning, and, in one instance, a falling meteorite. The thieving, corpulent Mayor swore that he would not be taken and spent the day in his chambers surrounded by guards and a large, ticking pendulum clock. He sweltered at his desk, pretending to study official documents. He had already filed for his seventh reelection campaign. At five minutes before midnight, one of the guards rushed past the others and stabbed him in the heart with a dagger.

The renegade guard, who had lied about his death date on his employment application, knew that he himself would perish that night: this certainty had given him the courage to strike against civic corruption. In the melee, he was shot to death by the other bodyguards. A minute later a second intended assassin burst through the skylight, dangling from a rope, surprised by the carnage below. The bodyguards fired on him as well.

As for the warden, his long life was oddly uneventful, hollow between the firm walls of its birth and death dates. No further executions were ordered by the city's courts, for it was presumed that the deaths of capital criminals had already been arranged. The warden married a woman whose life would last nearly as long as his, and they had children who, like everyone else born after Ganz's execution, grew up without the foreknowledge of their death dates. His children knew about the curse, of course, but for them it was some kind of mythic abstraction, a certain philosophical stance toward the future, essentially morbid. The warden's decline was gradual; after his eightieth year, he was almost constantly aware of some pain or discomfort. The remaining thirteen years were like a scorched desert that he was forced to cross on his knees. In that interval he had many occasions to think of the murderer Lester Ganz and his evil legacy to the city. Or perhaps the legacy wasn't entirely evil, the warden concluded, or perhaps it was no more evil than the other physical constants of existence that governed our lives.

After the old warden passed away, a few men and women subject to the curse were still left, but they too went to their graves (which had been excavated in advance) and by that time the city had long discontinued its quixotic use of the 730-day calendar. Yellowed and torn copies were collected as folk art souvenirs, their purposes vaguely recalled as superstitious. A graduate student at the state university wrote a paper that went unpublished. The life insurance industry gradually restored itself. Once the mechanisms of the anniversary gift watches fell apart, no one knew that they had once run backward. Even before the last children of the cursed generation had expired, the city's people had returned to normal life, selling and buying, teaching and learning, killing and birthing, hating and loving, as if the days of their deaths could not be imagined at all.

FACTITIOUS AIRS

Given the long, bloody history of my gingivitis, I go in for a periodontal cleaning every three months, and every time the experience is as it was before: the upholstered chair, the pleasantries with the attractive blond hygienist, the blood pressure check, the tender removal of my eyeglasses, the clasp of the rubber Groucho Marx nose, the first sweet fragrances of nitrous oxide, my jokey but desperate appeal that the supply be turned up. Before I've even tasted the gas, I'm visited by the sense that nothing exists beyond the wallpapered ramparts of the treatment room and that the whole of eternity is composed of a single periodontal cleaning, which I may anticipate, experience, and recall simultaneously.

Nitrous is not strictly necessary for a routine gum cleaning, but I demand it because I know from past cleanings, and perhaps from those yet to come, that the gas will produce some potently intoxicating effects. I believe these effects may be capable of giving me distance from myself and the mind-numbing realities of my everyday life. With this distance, I may be able to think more imaginatively about several personal, professional, and philosophical conundrums and problems. Before today's visit to the periodontist, I've rehearsed a series of questions that I would like to consider during the procedure. I've prepared an agenda before previous cleanings, but this time I'm firmly resolved to address it.

"Open. Turn this way."

A circle of pure white radiance, the reflection of a ceiling lamp, passes before my eyes as the hygienist inserts a dental mirror into my mouth. I inhale through my nose, still waiting for the gas to take effect. The hygienist's head comes close. My eyes roll up to look into hers, which are contact-lensed and focused on the interior of my lower mouth. She surveys the much-worked-over terrain. The mirror unintentionally taps a tooth. The touch is transmitted, muffled, to the tooth's interior nerves, but the outside of the tooth remains insensitive to the device itself. I take in another lungful of nitrous.

Her next instrument, a sickle-shaped probe, follows the path of the mirror and touches down on some tissue gently. It pauses to collect itself before finding its way between my teeth and the gum line. The hygienist starts to remove the accumulated gunk that has collected there. The scraping hurts at first, yet the discomfort becomes increasingly irrelevant as the gas bubbles into my bloodstream and diffuses through my nervous system. I'm aware of the discomfort, of course. I'm aware of everything. But mostly, as the gas takes hold, I'm aware of my awareness. That is the first effect of the "factitious airs," as nitrous oxide was called by the Scottish inventor James Watt in the eighteenth century, and I congratulate myself for recognizing the effect. My awareness has almost tangible substance and can be picked up and turned around and scrutinized, if I can only find the words to describe it.

Yet words fail. I *can't* describe it. Language simplifies our experience. I'm imprisoned by cliché, by shorthand, and by metaphor. The phrase *distance from myself*, which I employed earlier, is a figure of speech, not an actually possible condition. I recall that I should work on my agenda.

The gas is deepening its effects now. The probe reaches into a gappy region in my lower right mouth, finding something there, some debris or a particle, and pushes it from its place. The particle can be measured only in microns, yet I recognize by its removal the minute pressure the particle has been exercising against the gum for weeks. I become keenly aware of the contours of its absence. My thoughts come swiftly: the probe, the particle, an idea about a conversation I had with a friend three years ago, a notion about a book I once hoped to write, a qualification of my theory about the limitations of language. And I see that just as one's ordinary life is framed by sober reality, so too are these elevated perceptions framed by the nitrous oxide. I may step back, look at these thoughts and list them, but I'm doing so only from within yet another, slightly larger frame of reference. I strain now to make myself aware of that frame, and then strain to see beyond it. At the same time, something weird happens, or perhaps that thing happens first and *then* I strain to see beyond the frame.

What happens is this: I become aware of a certain vital sound, a sound of unsurpassed strangeness that I always hear at some point during my gum cleaning, something mechanical or electronic, a robotic, deep croaking sound, an actual voice that pronounces a series of discrete syllables. It signals an entrance into something, or a beginning or a deepening. But I can't in any way identify the syllables or transliterate an approximation of the consonants and vowels that compose the word, if it is a word, if even the idea of a word is too ordinary to describe what I've just heard. This group of sounds, perfectly audible but unrepeatable, implants itself in my consciousness.

I'm thrilled by the weirdness, the first indication that I've gained access to another frame of reference. At the same time, I'm aware that ordinary terrestrial music is being piped into the treatment room where my corporeal self is having his gums cleaned. This is what I hear: Frank Sinatra, belting out "Bim Bam Baby." The Axel Stordahl arrangement is actually pretty great, and I wonder if I'm hearing it within the same reality as the one in which the unfamiliar, unworldly nonmusic is being made, or if this is even the correct way of asking the question. Is it ever possible to break through the structure of everyday thinking, especially while someone is removing your dental tartar?

I entertain the thought that this experience may serve as the basis for a short story, which will feature an unnamed protagonist much like myself (the speculations, the gingivitis). Most of the story will take place inside his head. He will enter a new world of perception. Certain truths will reveal themselves to him. The story will be typeset in a familiar roman font and printed on familiar acid-free paper cut and sized in a familiar rectangular shape. I begin its composition, if not finding the words, then at least hearing an echo of the sounds that the words may make in a potential reader's ear. As the nitrous occupies an ever-larger portion of my consciousness, however, the idea falls away. The ambition becomes offensive. Writing about the experience will simply conventionalize it. At its best, the story may suggest some of the mystery that hovers around our encounters with material reality, but it will never truly describe this heightened sensitivity to the transcendent. I should find some better use for my enlightenment than publication, the same banal, quotidian ambition that I carry with me all the time in the months between periodontal appointments.

Other patients in the large dental practice are inhaling nitrous oxide at this very moment, located somewhere within another frame of reference or on another plane of being; or rather, located on *this* plane of being, right down the hall. Can we possibly detect each other? Can we make contact over the heads of our hygienists? Hello, hello? Indeed, hundreds of people in this city, in other dentists' offices, are simultaneously under nitrous. I concentrate on reaching out across this plane, not only to the nitrous-intoxicated citizens of the city, but beyond, unrestricted by geography, to dental patients all over the world, and to those inhabiting other worlds too. The thought is followed by the conviction that, yes, I *can* see these patients: they are untethered spirits, buoyed to the upper reaches of this higher realm, even if their mouths or other feeding apertures are open, drooling, on the surfaces of the spheres far below.

And when we meditate in unison, as we join together in our supramental community, what are we thinking? I can't say, not because I don't know—I know it as intimately as I know my name, and as I now know my true *secret* name—but because what we think together is beyond the workaday language that men and women employ to describe tiny, pitiful non-nitrous reality.

At that moment I become aware that in the distant periodontal office, where my body lies like a prehistoric artifact, another hygienist has entered the room. She too is blond and she may have cleaned my gums once before. She's wearing the usual shapeless scrubs, except they're made of what looks like silver lamé. Also, some strange, glowing, tubular mechanism is wrapped around the back of her head.

"I'm back," she says.

Not looking up, my hygienist asks if she's returned from a certain place. She says "from," followed by a sound, evidently a place name, that can't be approximated by any established alphabet or rendered by the normal human speech apparatus, like the robotic voice I heard earlier. The place she identifies is somewhere unknown to earthly mapmakers, yet I recall now that it was spoken of last time I was in the dentist's chair.

"Yes, I was there for two billion years."

"That was some vacation then."

"Not really a vacation," the second hygienist says, sighing, apparently lifting the appliance from her head. Then I realize that she's removed her entire head. Something may or may not emerge from between her shoulders in its place, something neither mechanical nor organic. Behind her, beyond the borders of a field of perception that I thought had dispensed with borders, I think I see the shadow of a vortex, if such a thing is possible. Speaking from the removed organ, which she's laid down next to my chart, she says, "It was exhausting. The entire time I was away I was intensely aware of the very fabric of the space-time continuum, from the large-scale structure of the universe to the lowliest quark. I finally understood how string theory can accommodate special relativity—duh-*uh!*"

"He has a deep pocket in number fifteen. Some bleeding."

"It's on his X-rays. I also realized that there is something beyond [that impossible-to-transliterate word again], something very far above and beyond. From that place, if you call it a place, the universe and all [????] seem to lie virtually on the same plane of existence."

I'm aware that I must be hallucinating; at the same time, I believe that the nitrous has impaired neither my senses nor my reasoning. My thoughts continue to come quickly, in logical order, and my ability to observe my surroundings has been improved, not diminished. I can read the time on my watch (3:27:56.0317) and distinguish, floating on my hygienist's right contact lens, a tiny speck shaped much like Kenya (though without Nyanza Province). I can appreciate that the silver lamé costume worn by the second hygienist is manufactured from fibers resistant to heat, cold, and other extraterrestrial rigors. I can also appreciate that the two hygienists are unaware that I'm attentive to the cosmic confidences they're exchanging.

It's questionable, then, who has access to a higher order of existence, me or the two hygienists, the second of whom has now restored her head to her body. With my now-more-encompassing sightedness, I recognize that possibly none of us do. It's possible that there is only a single order of existence, a single universe, and a single reality. The idea that reality comprises multiple layers, each more elevated than the one before it, may of course be a delusion, which I return to every time I go in for a periodontal cleaning.

Or perhaps the single-reality theory is simply the deadening assumption of everyday life, now imminent. The hygienists have adjusted the nitrous supply. The first whiff of pure oxygen is so powerful that I can taste its individual atoms, even run my tongue against the roughness in their atomic surfaces. But almost immediately that ability is lost, along with the memory of the atoms' texture. I'm aware that I've hardly worked on my agenda at all; or, rather, that I had briefly glimpsed something far greater than my agenda. After I inhale again, I find myself falling, falling through something—through *frames*?—and even these linguistic approximations demonstrate just how quickly my sensibilities are being dulled. The hygienist shifts in her chair and the springs half squeal, half squawk; I vaguely recall that I've heard that sound before, in radically different circumstances. It once meant something important. The next clear thought is disappointment with myself, for not working on the agenda, a sentiment that I recall from the conclusion of previous cleanings.

"You can rinse now."

Conventional reality is coming at me hard. Suddenly my mind slows down, or perhaps it has sped up, and I recognize that it's not a question of speed at all—another misconception. Only a single hygienist is in the room now, and she's wearing standard medical scrubs, whose details I will forget as soon as I turn away. "How do things look?" I ask, meaning the universe. But the question is meant to ask something even more than that, the particulars of which are rapidly fading.

She cleans my face. "Good, but we have to watch the pocket *here*." She taps the outside of my jaw. "Floss!"

There was a vortex, I think.

I no longer believe a second hygienist ever joined the first. Second hygienists are not usually present when I get my gums cleaned. Now the supposed conversation is fading from memory, regardless of the desperate effort I make to retain it. This is what happened last time too. The hygienist returns my eyeglasses, and the chrome medical furnishings within the room abruptly gain definition that I didn't know was lacking. At the reception area I pay my bill and make another appointment three months from today.

As I leave the office, the newly exposed surfaces in my mouth tingle with interdental awareness. I descend to the boulevard. Pedestrians jostle me, navigating the currents of foot traffic. Some make eye contact, briefly, and something's exchanged. Urgent conversations are under way. Also similarly urgent meditations and soliloquies. Some people walk the pavement on the verge of tears. Others have just realized that they've fallen in love. Everyone lives in a story. A baby in a stroller abruptly opens her eyes, surprised by the day. "The truth is . . .," one man says to another. I've returned to the world, which is no more comprehensible than it ever was.

IN BORGES' LIBRARY

A story haunts the library. It isn't known if the story is true, but we all understand that the value of a story doesn't depend on its being taken literally. The story concerns an aged reader who was stricken by a sudden lunacy and soon after that died. The other readers, or perhaps only a single reader, took note of his ravings, the most important of which, and the only one that has survived the generations before me, was this: the last book he read proved that everything he had read before it was read *wrong*. His life had been wasted.

It's difficult to imagine a madman in these rooms; certainly a raving one wouldn't be tolerated. You try to imagine a disruption in the placid order of readers at their tables, their books open before them, and can't; you try to imagine the moist, sharp, deep-time smell of old books replaced by the particular odor produced in a seizure's sweat, and fail; most of all, you wonder what a shout or scream would do here. Would it echo from the varnished walls forever or would it disappear, leaving a silence even more intense than this? The madman was put to bed. The library's delicate volumes have to be kept from danger; its patrons have to go on with their reading. Concentration is demanded. Unless I look away from the book before me, I can't tell the color of the carpeting. The rooms are softly lit by table lamps; you associate the sun with mental illness.

No one knows the title of that astounding last book the madman read. The librarian-housekeeper, perhaps an ancestor of the woman who today delivers us our books and serves us our tea, did not save the request slip. The book, she told one reader bold or perverse enough to question her, was returned to the stacks, and she couldn't recall where.

It was perhaps that unusually inquisitive reader who undertook a search of this library that has neither a card catalog nor any sort of listing of books about the proper apprehension of literature that might include a title whose thesis was so radical it would craze and kill its readers. A survey of certain works that, it was thought, might refer to the other, deadly work proved fruitless. Shortly (in the time of the library this could mean decades or generations), it came to be believed that the book being looked for was not necessarily about the act of reading. Perhaps it wasn't the book's content, but the presentation of its content, that destroyed the old man. The scope of the investigation widened; texts were again combed for references, clues, rumors. This time a few potentially relevant citations were discovered, but they were to several books, and no consistent and independent references were strong enough to indict any single work. In any event, it was unclear what would have been done with the book if it had been found.

I think belief in the circumstances of this story has waned, though in the library there is no way of knowing what another reader believes or, for that matter, how he or she reads. This is why the story is so credible. No one knows how the old man read or what he did with his books at all. It's impossible, I believe, for one reader to communicate to another how he has read a book at the level where the book is most intimately experienced. It's possible that we all read wrongly and this single book lies in wait on the shelves, waiting to tell us so, and will pick us off one by one, or that we all read correctly and only the old man read wrongly and we have all read the book already and thought it unremarkable. Or that we each read wrongly in a different way and there's a different mortally wounding book for each of us.

This is what haunts us, quietly and individually. I don't know what my neighbor reads; nor would I ask her. I do know, however, that she broods over this story. Or perhaps she doesn't even know this story. Perhaps I've made it up and told no one. I stand in the last reading room, at the doorway, and the housekeeper is about to ask me for my request slip. I can't go past the doorway into the stacks, but I can peer down the crammed galleries and obliquely see in their doorways the books of other galleries extending into dimness like the image of one mirror in another. Book-lined staircases stretch above and below. I take a deep breath before returning to my reading, inhaling nothing but the decomposing elements of read and misread books.

TEACH YOURSELF TSILANTI: PREFACE

With grave humility and unalloyed pleasure, we present this brief instructional manual for the Tsilanti language, a noble, penetratingly expressive tongue whose long-perished native speakers were the inhabitants of a country that no longer exists on a continent that for all intents and purposes has been misplaced. We have pieced together its elements from secondary medieval sources, scraps of bills of lading, and old legal documents, most of them forgeries, as well as traces of Tsilanti influence in modern languages that, interestingly, have no philological relationship with Tsilanti. It has been the work of a lifetime.

We know little about the Tsilanti people, save for their language. Given the frequency of certain words found in the surviving records, they may have been a nation of herders or traders, or perhaps acrobats, or simply men and women who, staring from their windows onto whatever terrain distinguished the territory of Tsilantia (if that was what they called it), occupied their lives wondering how to make a living, promising to get serious about it tomorrow. We have established, however, that Tsilanti was predominantly a language of romance. Its poets composed the most heart-breaking lyrics ever heard, sung beneath open balconies in cobblestoned Tsilanti cities that now lie under office towers and shopping malls. Their songs were addressed to maidens simultaneously chaste and seductive, modest and alluring, remarkably so in their full-length veils. Perhaps this is one reason why students of Tsilanti always find themselves on the verge of sweet heartbreak. Tsilanti poetry was accompanied by six-stringed lyres whose precise sounds have never been replicated.

The average person—say, Aurora, the comely barista who works Wednesday through Saturday from three to seven P.M. at the Café Phoneme—is unaware of the world's rich Tsilanti cultural heritage. But this person can be introduced to the language, her life enriched by the acquisition of a few words per day. The initial purpose of Tsilanti instruction is not immediate fluency, for what is the hurry in articulating our Tsilanti-inflected sensibilities? Rather, let us come to understand and appreciate the Tsilanti way of life, and immerse ourselves in it completely.

As the student will shortly discover, Tsilanti has thirty-one separate words that can represent the English word *speech*, but none for *silence*. A native speaker would argue, if he could possibly understand what we mean by silence, that there is no such thing as silence, only no-talk, no-sigh, no-birdsong,no-hum-of-commuters-murmuring-on-the-platform-as-they-wait-for-their-morning-train.

The written language of the Tsilanti has been lost. All we know about the Tsilanti alphabet is that it contained between eight and twelve letters, and four subscript intonation indicators, all of which could be combined to make more than sixty distinct sounds, several outside the range of normal human hearing. The system of phonetic spellings in the following pages is approximate—more of a suggestion than a rule.

Aurora says she is part-Livonian, part-Basque, part-Khazar, and part-Okinawan, a typical twenty-first-century mélange, yet we detect qualities that may once have been considered Tsilanti in her lustrous eyes, full lips, and unabashedly sharp nose. She moves with a classical dancer's fluttery grace between the register and the espresso maker. Every few minutes she determinedly pushes her hair back from her eyes. With unfeigned friendliness, she takes orders for caffeinated drinks from customers with whom she is not as familiar as she is with us. All this testifies to a Tsilanti background, or if not a background, then at least an affinity with Tsilanti manners.

Aurora has resisted our perhaps feeble attempts at banter and can't recall any of the Tsilanti words related to her work with which we have tried to supply her (for instance, the words for cup, for saucer, for brew, for skim mochaccino). It is difficult to teach a foreign language over a coffee counter, of course, and so far Aurora has declined offers of private instruction, or even to say whether she is available to meet in the hours when she is not performing her duties at the café. We hope that she will accept a gift of a copy of this book in the spirit with which it is offered.

The spirit is purely Tsilanti. How did Tsilanti gallants win their sweethearts? Not with testosterone-fueled competitive violence, nor with gaudy displays of material riches, nor with glib lines of poetry ripped off from professional bards. No, the currency of love in the era of Tsilanti greatness was manufactured by patient, passionate, intimate instruction. The Tsilanti swain approached his maiden with fresh or obscure words, phrases, and sentences. With his glamorous baubles of language, he gave her a new way of thinking about the world and the distinct items that populate it. If she accepted his tribute, the Tsilanti couple began to share a common experience, a vision, and a life. This is all any of us can hope for within the span of our brief earthly tenures.

The reader will note interspersed among the lessons a number of delicate line drawings, yet to be commissioned, which demonstrate Tsilanti's dependence on hand signals to carry meaning. For example, the complicated six-syllable word that indicates the desire for peace signifies the opposite when the right palm is fully extended without the thumb retracted, a careless error that has caused much intra-Tsilanti strife, and eventually led to the destruction of the Tsilanti people. These sketches should be given extra attention. The sweet, gentle word that expresses maternal love can also mean automobile carburetor if not accompanied with a tug of the right earlobe. The gestures should be practiced daily, as we often do at our table by the café window, observing our reflection in the glass, for hours. Appreciating the artistic touch with which Aurora swirls the outline of a heart in the espresso's crema, we're certain that she will illustrate these hand signals with distinctive charm, once she's asked.

Tsilanti is not the only mode of speech that has disappeared from human lips, tongues, and palates; it is only the most beautiful. Every year the last native speaker of one venerable language or another mumbles his final prayers and takes the language with him to the other side of existence. Farewell, Corsican! Good-bye, Cappadocian Greek! Take it easy, !Kung! *A hui hou*, Hawaiian! *Zai gezunt*, Yiddish! Expiring languages may be mourned and their carcasses studied, but the resurrection of the greatest of them is the task of this book's editors and the challenge taken on by the diligent student.

Courage is required to learn a new language, especially a language that is not spoken by more than one other living person. Faith is required as well: in the communicability of elusive thoughts and sentiments and in their receptivity. Yes, faith is required. The persevering, hardworking student will someday find herself speaking Tsilanti with fluency and ease, with illuminating eloquence, and with wit and sincerity and uncommon intelligence. When that day comes, she will have been changed irrevocably. We are confident that she will then speak the words that will express her truest self and see, for the first time, the face of her truest love.

"CITY OF SPIES"

Christoph Czarnecki loves Z., this city of cafés, tuxedoed waiters, wide boulevards, and high medieval walls, and he envies Darryl Davidson his permanent position here. He suspects Davidson of biasing his reports—perhaps by raising doubts about Ephraim Ettinger—in order to maintain his post and wonders if he himself would be capable of the same duplicity, for the same reason. He could make a strong case against Davidson. After all, Davidson was seen in a café with Fingerman just the other day. Ettinger is assigned to watch Fingerman; Czarnecki might reasonably claim that the purpose of Davidson's rendezvous with Fingerman was to compromise Ettinger's operation. Of course, the meeting might have been entirely innocent, but Czarnecki could emphasize its impropriety, thereby demonstrating that his own continued presence in the city is critical.

On the other hand, Czarnecki must suspect the ease with which his operatives learned of the meeting and the wealth of details in the report. The two men took a window table; during the long interview, according to the report, Fingerman had a beer, a sausage, three espressos, part of a strudel, and then a cognac. Czarnecki wonders if he's being tested, to determine which interpretation he will place on the meeting. Someone acting in concert with Davidson and Fingerman may be hoping to maximize his own importance by undermining confidence in *Czarnecki's* credibility.

Czarnecki paces the faded carpet in his hotel suite, relights his pipe, and gazes through the thick, leaded window into a tangle of trolley cables wrapped in the gauze of dusk. On his desk lies Davidson's skeptical evaluation of Ettinger's accusations against Fingerman. Czarnecki recalls Godel's incompleteness theorems: a mathematical system cannot be validated solely within the terms of the system. Sticking to a given set of axioms, its theorems will either generate contradictions or truths that are unprovable. A corollary applies to espionage. An agent's loyalty cannot be proven merely on the basis of his reports. You must make a judgment based on surveillance of the agent, compiling intelligence that will go into a report that must in turn be evaluated by someone else, who will require surveillance of you.

According to Ettinger's report, Davidson says, Fingerman claims that Goldinski is loyal. Ettinger, however, charges that Fingerman has destroyed the evidence against Goldinski. Davidson says that Ettinger is lying; that Ettinger has, in fact, attempted to compromise Goldinski. But if Davidson knows that Czarnecki knows he's met with Fingerman, he must assume that Czarnecki will use that information to support Ettinger. Davidson, Czarnecki reasons, must know then that Goldinski is indeed loyal and expects that Czarnecki will be discredited by backing Ettinger, thereby undermining any charges against Davidson himself.

Czarnecki leaves the hotel and from a call box at the outskirts of the city telephones Goldinski. Without identifying himself, Czarnecki offers him conclusive evidence against Hilbert that, he tells Goldinski, is actually false. He then posts a recording of the conversation to Fingerman. Ettinger, he knows, will intercept the tape, preventing Fingerman from protecting Goldinski, if Goldinski accuses Hilbert. Davidson will continue to discount Ettinger's charges and will be discredited when the charges are confirmed. But Hilbert's phone is tapped; Goldinski's suite has been searched; Fingerman's secretary has betrayed him; Ettinger's wife has been indiscreet; Davidson's files have been stolen; Czarnecki has been followed from the hotel by a busboy. Documentation is enclosed. Christoph Czarnecki returns to his writing table in his hotel suite and stares through thick, leaded windows out into the city, where other spies sit at their writing tables in their hotel suites, staring through thick, leaded windows out into the city.

—B.

SQUARE PAUL-PAINLEVÉ

As a young man I spent some time in Paris. Much of this time was consumed in the city's more modest public parks. Avoiding the great green agoraphobia-inducing spaces such as the Jardin du Luxembourg and the Bois de Boulogne, I passed my afternoons occupying park benches in the small and enclosed neighborhood squares that are hidden away in every quarter of the city. I studied the parks' other visitors and imagined their interior lives, sometimes in minute detail. On these afternoons I also engaged in a great deal of introspection about my own life, deeply contemplated the mysteries of human compulsion, and developed some ideas and theories distinguished by their varying degrees of outlandishness.

I knew no one in Paris and spoke no French.

While in such philosophical contemplation one afternoon I gradually became aware of something strange taking place within Square Paul-Painlevé. The small fifth-arrondissement park, entered through a gate on the rue des Écoles, by the Sorbonne, was named after the mathematician who twice served the Third Republic as prime minister. This was my favorite place to sit, in part for its striking bronze sculpture depicting the legendary she-wolf who suckled the infant twins Romulus and Remus.

That gray, mild winter afternoon my attention was directed toward the bench in the corner of the square closest to the Cluny excavations. Over the past few days I had come to suppose that something was wrong with this bench, perhaps a loose slat or a protruding nail: vague signs of distress would almost always appear on the faces of the men and women who sat there. Oddly, these visitors remained on the bench despite their evident discomfort, though when they finally left, it was often with a nearly violent abruptness.

Only now after further observation did I realize that these departures occurred when another person came to sit alongside the first person. The first person's expression of impatience and distress would vanish and he would virtually spring from his seat and, after collecting his things, dash from the park.

From these observations I developed an admittedly baroque theory: that the bench was somehow enchanted and that this enchantment compelled whoever occupied it to remain there until relieved by someone else.

In this unending cycle the bench was never empty, not even at nightfall. It occurred to me that over the past several decades thousands of Parisians, tourists, and soldiers of occupying armies had been caught in this sorcery, but they had never revealed their victimization to anyone.

Perhaps the promise of joining such a secret society, even one whose members did not know each other's identities, persuaded me to move from my comfortable, ordinary park bench. I chose a particularly opportune moment: on the pavement near the wolves two young boys in scarves and mittens, evidently brothers, had begun a mock sword fight with sharpened sticks. Their horrified au pair, imprisoned on the corner bench, cried out, *"Non, non, non!"* She had desperately tried to lure them back moments before by shaking a brown paper bag of sweets at them. Almost casually, I strolled across the park and took my place alongside the woman, who was then free to intervene in the skirmish. She hurriedly pulled them from the park.

I settled onto the bench and was immediately disappointed. The bench was not uncomfortable at all and I experienced neither an impulse to flee nor to stay. It was an ordinary bench. I was reminded now that I was often carried away by fantastic conjecture.

Nevertheless I remained. Although nothing had happened to restrict the operation of my nerves and muscles and I was perfectly free to rise from the bench and go on my way, I didn't rise. I knew that I was in no way being compelled by the *bench*; rather I compelled myself to continue sitting there, as if to justify my original speculation.

As I wondered how long I would choose to stay, I observed a softening of the afternoon light, the first intimations of evening. Soon I would have to leave, or perhaps I should leave now. Time was passing furiously and with this realization came the conviction that in fact I was unable to rise from the bench. I had not yet formed a definite wish to leave, but I was sure I was trapped, just as everyone before me had been trapped. I thrilled at the thought.

My thrill turned to anxiety as evening deepened and the park emptied of visitors. I hadn't yet tried to leave. I wondered if the not-trying was the occult mechanism that detained me. There was no weight on my body and nothing wrong with my legs. Yet I remained, waiting for someone to occupy the other part of the bench. I understood now that my chance of being relieved would drop off as the temperature fell and that I could be forced to spend the entire night in the park. I would have to wait until the park filled the next morning and someone consented to share the bench with a disheveled young man. Otherwise, I would be condemned to spend another frigid night outside, becoming more disheveled, and remain there indefinitely. The park bench was a destiny with which I had been flirting for years.

As my predicament became clearer, I was suddenly rescued from it. Someone appeared and, despite the number of empty benches in the park, this person sat beside me. Before I could savor the full taste of my bondage, I was free. I almost regretted it. Just as I leaned forward to rise, I glanced over at the new arrival—and then I fell back.

She was a lovely young Frenchwoman, a girl no older than I was. In the particularities of her features, her beauty was distinct; at the same time she was an anonymous member of the species of such women who always passed me on the streets of the city oblivious to my existence. I saw them in the Metro, in the Gilbert bookstore, and in all the museums in the hours of free admission. I gazed down at her lap, where she had spread a small pile of books, all but one of them in French. The shocking exception, at the top of the pile, was published in my own exceedingly obscure native language: it was a meditation on romantic love.

Now I felt the girl's proximity like some kind of elemental force and was sure that she was keenly aware of my presence. I didn't stare, because I didn't want her to feel uncomfortable. Yet she didn't turn away, showing that she didn't feel the need to deflect my approach. I knew that if only I spoke with her, our future together would be ensured. Amazed at my good fortune, I began to frame my opening remarks in the language we evidently shared.

Before I could speak, however, I realized that, in order not to begin our relationship with a betrayal, my first duty to my intended sweetheart was to warn her of the unique properties of the bench on which we were sitting. Yet if I did so, she would flee, either from belief in my warning or, more likely and possibly more justifiably, from doubt in my sanity. Not only would I lose her, but I would remain trapped there for the night.

Thus my only possible action with the only woman in Paris who could have shared sympathies with me was to abandon her. Five or ten increasingly embittered minutes went by. Finally, I rose to my feet and without a word of acknowledgment or farewell hurried to the park gate. Night was falling like a thick gauze. As I looked back, the woman saw me and a faint absentminded smile played upon her face, the first microscopic glimmer of interest. I fled the park, never to love, and left this city of diverse enchantments the following day.

V. THE LARGE HADRON COLLIDER

The judge retired to his chambers, his brain buzzed by quanta and quarks, by muons and gluons, by bosons and hadrons—as well as by certain elusive iotas of jurisprudence.

The plea to issue an injunction that would halt the start-up of the world's largest particle accelerator was more vehement than the usual cases that shuffled their way into U.S. district court in Honolulu. The plaintiffs argued that while smashing subatomic particles at energies never before achieved on earth, the new Large Hadron Collider could inadvertently extinguish terrestrial life. Somewhere within the seventeen-mile-ring tunnel hundreds of feet below the Swiss-French border, in the maw of stellar forces and relativistic speeds, theoretically foreseen particle interactions could produce a small black hole that would swallow the planet. The other dread possibility was that the machine would create hypothetical particles called strangelets that, upon contact with other matter, would instantaneously turn the entire globe into the same material, all of it dead.

While the likelihood of either scenario was vanishingly remote, at the very most one in fifty million, the plaintiffs contended that the danger was so extreme, so total in its effects, that the project could not be allowed to proceed.

The judge gazed from his office window onto Honolulu Harbor, where the waves gently surged according to the rock-ribbed laws of classical physics. He knew something about these laws. He knew too of the heroic campaign to bring order to the anarchic realms of the subatomic. He sympathized with the scientists' quest to break down hadrons—composite particles like protons and neutrons—and find the mysterious Higgs boson, prove supersymmetry, and unearth deeply buried dark matter. In chance encounters within lightning-lit caverns on the other side of the world, the current model of the physical world would either be confirmed or discarded, and if discarded, then replaced by something more elegant and more legitimate. The more elegant the new model was—the more simply it covered the most complex phenomena—the more legitimate it would be; the law was like that too. You could support contemporary physics simply for its pursuit of elegance.

This case was an easy call. It was a nuisance lawsuit: the publicity-seeking fringe-science plaintiffs clearly had no legal standing, and the Hawaii district court had no jurisdiction, despite the federal monies that contributed to the

European project. The plaintiffs had filed it in Hawaii only because one of them lived here. If the judge issued an injunction against the scientists in Geneva, it would be dismissed on appeal, or even ignored, and he would be the subject of amused public commentary. The chance that he would decide in favor of the plaintiffs was therefore infinitesimal—even so, it was still many thousands of times greater than the chance that the Large Hadron Collider would destroy the planet.

The judge returned to his desk and flipped once more through the legal brief, not really studying it. He gazed for a moment through the open door to the outer office. He usually kept the door open, preferring to call for an assistant if he needed one. He also liked the bustle of the outer office. He didn't mind being distracted by the phones, by the murmur of professional and personal conversations, or by the clatter of the ink-jet printers. Sometimes a clerk or paralegal would pass the open door and he would look up.

He had recently become aware that, when he looked up, the paralegal he hoped to see was one of the new hires, an attractive recent UH graduate.

He heard her moving through the outer office right now, click-click-click, her heels like a metronome or a piece of scientific equipment, like, say, a particle detector. Tall and dark and shapely, the paralegal had been hired by Mrs. Bains;

the judge had nothing to do with it. The young woman had come in on her first day to introduce herself, her confidence as pronounced as her curves, and for a moment he felt small behind his desk, without authority at all. He reasserted himself, sitting in his chair a little taller, more judicial, fully professional, and entirely bland. Yet with a tiny, quick smile she somehow sent him a signal that she knew she had caught his eye. Or so he imagined. Weird, the judge told himself, and he went back to work. He saw her nearly every day over the next few weeks, often in what seemed to be a new outfit, in body-hugging blouses and above-the-knee skirts just *slightly* more showy than was typical in a federal-court office, particularly one as notoriously laid-back as the court in Honolulu.

The judge had spoken to her several times since then, gleaning some private details from her life and saving them like a child collecting pretty pebbles or shells from the beach. She had grown up in Vermont, where she had skied competitively; now she surfed competitively, longboard, on the North Shore. BA from Hilo, three years in the department of the state attorney general, criminal justice division. A fan of mai tais. A condo in Haleiwa. She intended to stay single. Chatting with him in the cafeteria checkout line, she had announced this last fact with what he now adjudicated could have been a wolfish grin.

Weird, he told himself again, but he also asked himself what his chances with her could be, as he seemed to do, instinctively, with every woman he met. The chances were always nil or close to nil. He was simply not that kind of guy and never had been, not even before he was married. Either he was not aggressive or not aggressive in the right kind of way, or he possessed insufficient desire, or he was truly faithful to his wife in heart and mind, or he didn't possess charm or the right kind of charm. The reasons were a mystery, as was the original mystery of why he was calculating his chances with her in the first place. He wasn't interested, not by a long shot. The tap of her heels faded as she left the outer office. He returned to the plaintiffs' brief.

The legal argument was weak, with few supportive citations from international or domestic law, but with many diversions down the byways of popular science, past Hawking radiation, Minkowski space, the Heisenberg uncertainty principle, and other speculations. Of these he had heard only of the Heisenberg uncertainty principle, which was hard enough to understand and believe. The theory maintained that the outcome of any quantum event, such as the decay of a radioactive particle, was not determined until the event was observed. Until then the particle apparently existed in every possible state, in a kind of cloud of possibility. This apparently had some bearing on the Large Hadron Collider.

One not-inelegant interpretation of the theory, which he may have read only in a magazine, suggested that there was no cloud at all. Something else was happening. If he understood the theory correctly, whenever a particle was confronted with a quantum choice, the universe copied itself, producing a new universe for every possible state of the particle. This occurred every moment a subatomic event was about to take place anywhere in the universe, an idea so preposterous that it wasn't included in the brief against the particle accelerator. The brief was presumably preposterous enough.

The judge considered the theory nevertheless. If he dismissed the case, and if this "many-worlds" or "multiverse" theory was correct, then on the day within a few weeks when the first particles in the accelerator were smashed, a multiplicity of universes would come into being. In nearly all of them terrestrial life would go on as it did before, with some provocative results garnered from the project, careers made, and Nobel Prizes won. But in one or two of those universes an earth inhabited by the judge and his loved ones would be annihilated, along with every trace of human history, including the science and legal dismissal that had engineered the annihilation. That world's Hawaii district court judge would experience a real, actual death—yet the world would be destroyed so quickly he probably wouldn't know it; nor would it be mourned by the copies of himself inhabiting the other universes.

Pacing his office, the judge returned to the window. Midafternoon traffic was starting to coagulate on Ala Moana Boulevard. He should file the dismissal and go home in time for a swim. He and his wife were attending a political dinner tonight. But uncertainty persisted at all levels of existence; you were immured in uncertainty. If every quantum event was subject to the many-worlds phenomenon, then you could suppose the same held true for the indeterminacies of human judgment. Whenever you made a choice, to attend law school or medical school, to wed or to stay single, to go back to the service line or to come in at the net, the universe responded. The judge would now either issue the injunction or reject the plaintiffs' plea, and at that moment the history of the universe would bifurcate, vulnerable to every consequence.

He raised his head from the brief. As if summoned into being by his most subterranean thoughts, or by the Large Hadron Collider itself, the new paralegal had appeared in the doorway to his office. She casually grasped the frame with both hands, occupying the entire doorway. Today she wore a slim, short, beige wrap dress. As she leaned forward in the doorway, the hem rode up a few inches farther. He observed the freshness in her eyes. Also, the openness and avidity of her expression, the untrammeled complexion, the carnivorous dentition. Also, the flat stomach, the powerful surfer's legs lengthened and tautened by her heels, a perfect line that terminated in her visibly elevated buttocks. The European particle accelerator was called the Large Hadron Collider, but every time he saw the word he read *hardon*.

"The Ninth Circuit called again." She winced in apology. The wince didn't mar her loveliness. "They really need you to get back to them before they close for the day."

"Right."

The paralegal flickered away into invisibility.

The judge's wife was a Democratic Party powerhouse, probably more influential than the state chairman. She had pulled the strings that had made him a federal judge. Other strings could be pulled, in the opposite direction.

He had been stalling for days. The Ninth Circuit's administrative offices needed him to finalize his arrangements for the judicial conference in Monterey the following month. Transportation, lodging, and the workshops in which the judge would be participating had to be decided. He also had to tell them which staff were accompanying him. He was supposed to bring a law clerk and a paralegal. Given the themes of the conference and her area of responsibility, the new hire was the obvious choice for the paralegal slot, almost the inevitable choice.

He knew how business-trip affairs were reputed to start: a late-night working dinner; seeing her back to her hotel room; a good-night kiss; a suggestion that they raid the minibar for a nightcap. A romantic involvement with the new paralegal in Monterey was anything but inevitable, but if he declined to bring her with him, it could be completely ruled out.

If the affair wasn't ruled out . . . if in fact it happened . . . and if the judge's wife discovered it . . . the potential consequences could be characterized only as cataclysmic. His wife would be furious. She would figure out ways to make him pay for it personally and professionally—and then politically, financially, physically, mentally, and spiritually, for decades to come, even after his death. And if the press found out, as they almost certainly would, the tortures would be multiplied like the image of his pain-racked self in two facing full-length mirrors. Reporters would go back and discover his every mediocre legal opinion and overturned decision, every half quid pro quo, every corner he ever cut, every trivial indiscretion, every speeding ticket. There had been a few too many gifts he had been too gracious to refuse.

But, oh, those heels, those legs.

A multiverse of multiple universes that survived the start-up of the Large Hadron Collider would contain many in which the new paralegal accompanied him to Monterey, offering her expertise on the criminal justice system. One evening, in some of those universes, he would walk the paralegal to her hotel room. In most of these universes, she would then gently rebuff his awkward advances; in a few she would repel him forcefully, with anger and indignation. He would have to apologize the following morning, pathetically. But in a couple of universes . . . he would enjoy carnal delights whose specificities and intensities he could now only imagine. Among the universes in which he frolicked with the new paralegal, unreservedly and triumphantly, there was at least one in which his wife didn't find out about it. That happy universe would seem to him—that judge—to be as solid and real as this federal court building in downtown Honolulu.

In *this* solid and real federal court building, the judge dismissed the case against the Large Hadron Collider and let the world take its chances. He completed the necessary paperwork, and all the possible outcomes ramified into newborn universes. He then called up on his desktop the file he needed to make the arrangements for next month's conference. He designated the flights to and from California that he and his team would be taking. He indicated which workshops he would be attending. He agreed to moderate a panel on judicial decision-making. For the closing luncheon he chose the salmon entrée. He would save the staffing assignments for last.

Part III
The Future

THE FUTURE

It rained (or is raining?) that morning, leaving the sidewalks gray and soft to the tread. The roads were (will be?) shiny and slick, and water droplets on passing cars and buses raced backward against the direction of human progress. The sky had cleared impeccably, without being forecast to do so. Passersby unbuttoned their raincoats and slickers. Moisture that remained suspended in the atmosphere threw up a gauze that beckoned to be torn away. Time coalesced into a single, crystalline nut, worn to a nuclear smoothness and bright as a thousand suns. Swift was (is?) visited by the sense that he was living in the past, that this instant had all the detailed and subtle temporal characteristics of *being* the past.

He was waiting at a bus stop, so wrapped up in his appreciation of the moment that minutes passed before he was aware of the company of three men in gray suits—businessmen; Swift's guess was followed by a subdued tremor of superiority. This was an era that privileged academia. The men did not appear to be traveling with each other, but they took turns pacing and hopping from the curb to the street, visibly embarrassed by their impatience. They rallied back at the pole and its red-and-white metal flag. Although the traffic was heavy, it moved fluidly, so it was foreseeable to Swift, who had become sensitive to what was foreseeable and what was not, that the bus would arrive shortly. As if he had already taken his seat, he scoffed at their anticipation.

A vague confluence of observations and events had impressed Swift as never before. All this was *old*, these fashions of clothing, these politically provocative haircuts (the idea that a haircut could *be* politically provocative), the unfashionableness of the Manhattan subprincipality in which he now rented a modest three-bedroom apartment, these treacherously shifting sexual mores. He turned from the street and examined the advertising in the window of the housewares store in front of which the route sign was planted. On an unremarked day not long ago, typefaces had been deprived of their serifs. Some rounding, bubbling, inflating process had gentled everything in the universe, including the appliances that the advertisements recommended, so that the ubiquitous, masculinely appended Bodonis and Times New Romans had been neutered, or at least been made androgynous (and *androgynous* was a newly fashionable word, with its own internally voiced seductions and provocations). Automobile bumpers appeared to have been softened and humanized; there was a romanticization of our public rhetoric, an embrace of the word *love* and an alternate, jaunty, pseudo-foreign spelling of it: *luv*. We were passing from the solidity implied by the serif. In the future, the material world would be less dense, bordering on the ethereal.

Although Swift was surprised at the uncharacteristic abstractedness of his thoughts, these thoughts did not now become more concrete. Was it possible for marijuana intoxication to be transmitted from one person to another through physical contact or mere proximity? Despite his squarish, murmured disapproval, his wife Jan had been experimenting with the drug, gliding through their shared space enveloped within a nimbus of pleasantly acrid fumes. This too seemed part of the past, even quaint.

Last week Swift had been intimidated. At thirty-two he was the youngest member of the Twenty-First Century Commission and, as an untenured associate professor, certainly the least garlanded. So far his only appearance on the stenographer's record had been an ironic remark attributed to the chairman, to the effect that Swift was Youth Personified. The stenographer, a squat, brassy-haired lady in a starched white blouse, paused to peer over her pince-nez, as if to verify his lack of age. The chairman followed this remark with a string of introductory sentiments:

- Forecasters commonly expected revolutionary advances in technology, yet they mistakenly limited their predictions of social change to extensions of current trends.
- Our future history should be conceived as a "multifold trend"; the concurrence of interrelated trends could be stochastically modeled. In other words, many variables were in play, and any predictions had to take into account their effects on each other. Outcomes could be expressed only in probabilistic terms.
- The commission's deliberations were meant to be heuristic, propaedeutic, and paradigmatic. *Heuristic* meant that these discussions were speculative. *Propaedeutic* meant that they were preliminary, with the expectation that fuller discussions would follow. *Paradigmatic* suggested that a model was being created for the conduct of further investigation.
- Three quarters of all Americans alive today were likely to live into the next century.

Swift would be alive, alert, and functioning, even rampant. Most of his colleagues on the panel, distinguished public-policy theorists and gray-faced professors reclining in named chairs, would not be. This gave him a certain significance, as if the commission were assembled in his behalf. Pipe smoke (tobacco) hung in soft blue clouds above the meeting table; bergs of ice fissured and fractured within pitchers of cold water; and a faint susurrus could be heard on the lips of dozing elders who would suddenly awake to interject brilliant reformulations not exactly to the point; all this was an artifact of another era. No one glanced Swift's way again.

He had aggressively planned his contribution to today's working session. Last night, while waiting for Jan to return home from some "all-girls party," Swift had drawn up a list of talking points, mostly having to do with the diminishing differences in urban, suburban, and rural politics, inevitable in a growing, urbanized, postindustrial society. This had been the subject of his acclaimed dissertation, which had won him the commission's notice in the first place. There were economic indices that could be tracked; demographic factors to be defined and quantified; technological innovations whose effects could be anticipated. Now the image of the vast megalopolis of the future lay before him, extending from Boston to Atlanta, a buzzing, hymenopterous complex of service-related commerce, a single nervy polity. He could hear its music and inhale its distinctive, not-yet-invented odors.

Struck by the solidity of this divination, with the observable traffic still busless, Swift savored the tenuity of the past-like present, its porousness and gossamer elusiveness. It was fundamentally naive—yes, even this (that) age of corruption and cynicism will someday be called innocent. The unusual eventfulness of the current week (dramatic political developments abroad; the rush to finish his latest submission to an influential policy journal; the occasion of Jan's perplexingly pointless untruth) remained abstract, a subterranean hum. Now various mood-inducing secretions spilled from his nostalgia glands, which seemed to be positioned behind his eyes on the upper anterior wall of his chronal cavity.

He felt happy, unaware that his life was about to change its course several times within the next ninety seconds.

The bus finally appeared at the avenue's vanishing point downtown, at the rim of the abbreviated urban horizon. Its imminence was somewhat disappointing. The future would come as surely as the bus; so would Swift's own passing.

He reflected that when you first looked at the second hand of a watch, you often couldn't detect its motion and supposed that you might have forgotten to wind it. But it would be seen in the following second to be moving smoothly without impediment. Like a second hand, the bus appeared paralyzed for an instant. And then, with the bus's advance, time rushed over him and he felt its coarse physical essence in his face—spongy, searing, and electric.

But now *motion* proved to be the illusion. The bus remained in the center of the roadway, mired between ticks. Swift gazed down the avenue, bewildered. Time itself was stopped there; a patch of intermittently lined asphalt in Murray Hill was the dead center of the universe. Cars and trucks eddied around the bus and there was a flash of reflected light—the bus's glass door opening—and passengers were being disgorged onto the street like a line of guppy eggs. He realized at last that the bus had broken down.

He smiled wanly. His new concern was about being late, and the embarrassment that would be consequent when he entered the commission's meeting room while one of his senior colleagues was speaking. The men would be arrayed around the lion-clawed mahogany table that had occupied the paneled chamber since the beginning of the current century. Swift would be watched as he withdrew his notebook from his unmarked (it was new, a gift) untenured associate professor's briefcase. He foresaw this. He teetered on the curb. Each of the businessmen had already stepped into the street to look for the next bus and had returned to the pavement. They were wondering whether they should hail a cab. Now Swift sensed that it was his turn.

Although the traffic was moving quickly, it had retained its rush-hour volume. Swift left the curb just as there was a break in the two near lanes. In doing so, he ignored the theorems of New York road dynamics that he had patiently acquired since his arrival in the city. A beer truck noisily shuffled up the center lane, falling behind the ambient traffic—Swift should have been aware of how the truck distorted the vehicular flow. The first bar of the beer's Wagnerian advertising theme foamed in his ears. At that moment (it was all a single moment), a small, red car darted from behind the truck in a reckless effort to pass it.

It was too late for Swift to retreat. In any event, he was as immobilized as the bus that was stranded down the avenue and the second hand located in hypothesis. The car loomed. He jerked up his right leg and perched on tiptoe, like a flamingo, his argyle socks showing. His future seemed to have been compressed into the volume of a thimble. Yet the earth continued its motion around the sun. Safely on the sidewalk, two girls in parochial-school uniforms consumed their push-up ice-cream pops and resolved not to return to school after lunch. They would take the subway to the Village. The beer truck moved uptown. *It's not bitter, not sweet. It's the dry-flavored treat*. And this moment no longer seemed like the past, but rather like a burning droplet of the excruciating present.

And he was not dead, his pulse thumped in his ears and the fumes of smoking rubber scorched the interiors of his nostrils. The bumper came to rest at his knees, a kiss when he least expected it. In response to the shriek of the tires that Swift never heard, pigeons resting on the pediment of a bank across the street lumbered into the air, and on the next block the shoulder of a long-haired youth's blue denim shirt was soiled by one of them. He was on his way to Swift's apartment. The young man brushed off the guano and wiped his hand along the side of his jeans. Swift was now astonished by the conditionality of a fact that only a few moments earlier he had taken for granted: that he would attend the meeting of the commission.

He stared at the car's windshield. Reflected upon it, a ghostly shop-sign advertised XƎMIT wristwatches. Swift became aware of the sound of human distress. He looked beyond the reflection and saw that the driver of the automobile was in tears, her hands balled at her face.

Swift finally succeeded in putting himself in motion. He scurried around to the open window on the passenger's side of the car—the traffic whizzed by on the other side—and bent low, both hands gripped around the handle of his attaché case. "It's my fault!" he declared gallantly. "My fault entirely. And look, no harm was done!"

The driver's face ran with tears, which dripped onto her skirt and beaded there. Swift was transfixed by the skirt: by its brevity and by its twenty-first century pink vinyl sheen.

Also by the young woman's slender, pale legs. And that she too was a particular of the past. She sobbed, "I can't drive in this city!"

Swift leaned into the car, and her face seemed to spin toward him. It bore a nearly pre-Cambrian freshness. Her liquid brown eyes were surrounded by a muddied delta of purple eyeliner. She had gnawed her lips, leaving them blanched. "Don't be silly," he said. "Of course you can. You were driving perfectly all right."

"I can't!" she insisted. "The taxis don't signal, the buses break down in the middle of the road, no one stays in their lanes—and the pedestrians don't stay on the sidewalk! I'm leaving the car here!"

"It'll get towed," he forecast, alarmed.

"I don't care. It's better than getting killed!"

"I suppose," he said, having had his car towed once. He studied her as if she contained some secret about the era in which they lived. The young woman's accessories announced the date as bluntly as the line across the top of the *Times*: these specific hairpins, necklace, and bracelets. The hair-style that flattered her face now wouldn't in four years; they would laugh, embarrassed, at the photographs. With a jolt, Swift realized that they inhabited (inhabit, will inhabit) not an arbitrary moment from which the commission proposed to view another arbitrary moment: this was, rather, the historical brink. He and the girl lived in an age whose possibilities were unfathomed by his colleagues on the commission. Changing mores and modalities. Multifold trends. The Pill. That had a lot to do with everything. Doomed not to reach the millennial marker, the odometer's ascending clutch of goose eggs, most of his colleagues could not appreciate this. The one thing you could never fully predict is getting old.

Swift asked her, "Where are you going?"

"New Rochelle," she said, weeping.

These two words electrified him. Asking the question, he had expected without reason that she would announce a destination convenient to his own. But New Rochelle was far, far better. It would be impossible to return in time for the meeting of the commission. Playing hooky: now, *that* was a trend that hadn't been stochastically modeled, yet it defined the era. A soaring vision of potentialities and concurrences was joined to a mighty adolescent rush of blood to his extremities. His absence wouldn't be noticed.

"If you like, I'd be happy to drive you."

"To New Rochelle?"

"I can take the train back."

She stopped sobbing and her face brightened, as if powered by a newly developed energy source: solar, wind, fusion . . . The suddenness of the transformation revealed not only her youthfulness, but also the volatility of contemporary conditions. Swift became aware that all this time the car radio had been on, and he identified the booming voice of the aggressively familial disc jockey. The young woman didn't reply at once, and Swift remained crouched at the door of the vehicle. His posture was characteristic of the era, as was the resolution of these events, already located in the legendary past. Swift and the girl turned away from each other and looked far up the long, broad avenue, where the day's normally heavy traffic, conveying the present moment's diverse freight, was dissolving (dissolved, will dissolve) into the thin, light-blue haze of a future that had so far been left unencumbered.

MERCURY

My job as an elementary-school teacher ended abruptly after eight weeks. Walking heavily to my car, I was devastated, but I recognize now that I was never cut out to be a teacher, for reasons that have nothing to do with the circumstances of my departure. While I don't regret my lost career in education, the circumstances continue to puzzle me. They gnaw at me, sometimes. They may even amuse me. Over the years, in my quiet hours of contemplation, usually in the car, when I've wondered why my life went one way and not another, or why what is now widely obvious about the multiformity of human sentiment was not clear then, I've employed guesswork and imagination to reconstruct that strange, climactic afternoon. This is what I've come up with.

As is typical in grade school, lunch and recess that day were conducted unconscionably early, well before noon, I think, and the rest of the day stretched before my second-grade class like the voids of outer space. Room 112 had some heads-on-table "quiet time" and then a penmanship lesson, and I was beginning to understand that being a teacher could be as tedious as being a student. I instructed the kids, a few of them yawning or nearly dozing, to perform some writing exercises, but I could see, as clearly as if I were looking into an open pot, that the class was beginning to simmer and boil into general restlessness. Pencils rolled off desks. Ambitious doodling projects were undertaken. I myself was succumbing to an almost physically painful lassitude, and the desire to combat it seemed as urgent as if I were fighting for my life—or at least for my youth. I was just twenty-four. I paced the front of the room and smoothed my solid-blue tie, which, as an assertion of my independence, I kept unclipped. I knew it was a modest assertion. I stepped into the hallway for a moment, hoping that perhaps another teacher would have come out at the same time, for the same reason, and we could wave hello. No, the hall was empty. I went back to my desk. Aware that I was being more reckless now, I wrote a jesting, cryptic note to the lone friend I had acquired among my colleagues, a fifth-grade teacher, put it in a blank manila envelope, and called on one of the students to deliver it.

He was a slight, sallow boy, a boy named Sammy. He had finished his exercises several minutes earlier and had evidently fallen into a stupor so deep he was not even daydreaming. My calling of his name caught the mind of the class several moments before it caught his. Something must have heaved inside him then. He reddened. I tried to give him a reassuring smile, but he looked frightened by the attention he was suddenly receiving. I showed him the envelope. I leaned against my desk, waiting, and in the time it took me to get his attention, I reconsidered its contents. The boy rose like a rocket, very slowly, struggling to build power before he cleared the launchpad. Some of the girls in the class tittered.

"I need you to bring this to Mr. Harding," I said, suppressing my reservations. I tried to smile at the boy again. He didn't smile back, and I don't know if I ever saw him smile in the two months that I was his teacher, or if he ever raised his hand to answer a question. He was not the only shy child in the class, but I saw in him something especially vulnerable, perhaps a weak sense of his own self. If I had not lost my job, I might have reached him somehow. "Mr. Harding's in 212." I pointed at the ceiling above my head. "You know Room 212, right?"

Further sounds of amusement were generated by the question, or perhaps by his palpable, openmouthed dumbfoundedness. As a teacher, I had been reminded that elementary school was commonly hilarious, and anything, and especially another student, could provide a given minute's eyes-wetting, desk-pounding, falling-off-your-chair comedy. At the moment nearly every room in the building was located at some point on the continuum of burlesque, either in the dying climax of a joke or at the promising inception of a gag, or somewhere in the rise and fall of a prank. Any group of children, bright, vivacious, and bored, was charged with the potential for abundant mirth, not all of it good-natured.

Sammy took the envelope and small-stepped from the room, leaving my direct sight and entering into what is now the realm of my personal speculation, intuition, and sympathy. The hallway was cool and dim, shadowy and aqua-green, almost suggestive of the ocean's depths. His head finally cleared, or so he thought.

For the moment, having left the classroom, Sammy must have been elated: children cherish such puny notions about what constitutes freedom. In this particular school they were rarely allowed to walk the halls alone. The second-grade classes assembled in the playground, went to the lunchroom in a group, and at the end of the day filed from the building together. A second grader was permitted to leave for the bathroom only with a designated buddy, a degrading partnership that many of them had developed the physical stamina to avoid nearly every day of the school year. Now, as he passed the door to the first-floor boys' room on his own, Sammy was crossing a border. Everything looked new already.

This was a short-lived satisfaction, I suspect. He would have recalled the significance of his destination: the big kids' floor. His feeling of liberty shriveled away. The fifth graders were hard runners, tough talkers, pushers, shovers, fighters. They were trouble. In the hallways and in the playground, and on the way to and from school, Sammy would have tried to keep out of their lines of sight, so that he wouldn't be targeted for an abusive pleasantry or something worse. I had taken the class up to the 200s only twice this year, to Kevin Harding's room, to view two film strips unrelated to either his lesson plan or mine. My students understood that the fifth graders were disgusted by their presence.

Before he reached the stairs, Sammy would have gone by the principal's office, a glass-fronted suite of rooms at the end of the first-floor hallway. Although the office represented the ultimate punishment for severe disciplinary offenses, the school principal himself, Dr. Fairmount, styled himself as a figure of grandfatherly benevolence. Stout and balding, courteous and playful, he was said to know the name of every child in the building. On the day of Halloween the week before, he had toured the classrooms toga-clad as Zeus, cardboard lightning in one hand while he dispensed candy with the other.

Hallway passersby often discovered Dr. Fairmount in the front office, in a blue-gray business suit, amiably flirting with the office ladies. He may have seen Sammy through the glass that afternoon. If so, he would have smiled at him warmly, further impressing the ladies with his good nature.

The smile offered Sammy some comfort as he ascended the arduous big-kid stairs. He exhaled only when he arrived at the second floor, which, although it was the same dimensions as the first, seemed more commodious and wreathed in deeper, more alien shadows. His tiny footfalls resounded against the speckled tiles. As he checked each number above the rooms' entrances, he stepped back to the opposite side of the corridor, weaving down the hall like a drunk.

Most of the doors to the classrooms were left open. Even from a distance, by simply transiting the doorways, he attracted attention from the inattentive. He averted his eyes, so that he couldn't look in, maintaining his half confidence in the principle that what isn't observed can't observe, a mainstay of his everyday life. He passed 203 on the left, then 204 on the right. Two twelve would be down the hall and on the right, but he examined each door number anyway—another hedge, to ensure that he wouldn't become lost.

He eventually reached the correct room, where Kevin was at the blackboard. Kevin saw him the moment he appeared in his doorway, a tiptoeing wraith. Before the boy could even tap at the open door to ask for permission to enter, he was met by a wave of derisive jubilation from the fifth graders. His arrival was a surprise, an incongruity, the promise of a diversion, a delight, a gift that would make that dreadful hour of childhood go by. Sammy must have rocked back on his heels or made some other perceptible response because the first wave was followed by a no less vigorous second. The manila envelope trembled in his hand like a little bird. He had forgotten it was even there.

Kevin disregarded the commotion. He smiled kindly at the boy, but Sammy was hardly relieved. The fifth graders gazed at him with carnivorous pleasure. “Hello there, my friend,” Kevin said. “How can we help you?” The class celebrated again.

If only Sammy were capable then of recognizing that this glee, this bacchanalia, had nothing to do with him as an individual . . . It had nothing to do with him at all. In his shame, though, his body was immobilized while his mind, carried on tiny child-legs, frantically pursued through increasingly confined, dark rooms the small, verminous creature that might answer the question of why he was the object of ridicule. Why? Why? Why? The animal’s swishing, long tail led him into the grim chambers of his personal deficiencies, the recesses where his incompetencies lurked, past the crowded cell in which his many childish errors in thinking and deportment were held, and through a ragged hole into the crypt where dwelled restlessly his previous humiliations. He wondered what he should do. Under such scrutiny, he couldn’t check his fly. He weakly waved the envelope at the teacher.

Kevin motioned him in. He took a few steps and stopped. Kevin said, "Don't worry, we won't bite."

"Ha-ha-ha-ha-ha-ha."

The boy showed him the envelope again.

Kevin asked whom it was from. The boy could barely pronounce my name. Each stammer, blocked vowel, and blurred consonant provoked distinct notes of merriment that could be assigned to individual fifth graders. The sum of the class's response, a clattering-squealing noise that filled the room to the ceiling, comprised a multitude of pricks, jabs, and pinches, plus one or two disembowelments.

"He sent you? The envelope's for me?" Kevin said, his face crinkling in good cheer. The boy didn't respond. The teacher leaned over, resting his hands on his thighs. "Thank you. And what's *your* name?"

His name. Sammy could not bear the prospect of speaking his name. His name was a disgrace. He gazed across the room, focusing on a poster that illustrated the design of the new Mercury space capsule, the one-man vehicle that in orbit was an empire of perfect isolation. He recognized, sitting at desks below the poster, two or three of the fifth graders, big-brother versions of boys his own age who were indefatigably tormented by them. They looked at him with killing hostility. Several back-row girls grimaced in disdain; gum-chewing, hair-teased, sharp-tongued fifth-grade harlots, they were widely deemed capable of adult perversions. One whispered to her neighbor; the others giggled. This confirmed, as if confirmation were needed, that something was wrong with Sammy. He would spend the rest of his life trying to figure out what it was.

He said something that was unintelligible even to himself. This time Kevin chuckled. The teacher took the envelope, carefully lifted erect the clasp's silver angel wings, and removed a sheet of unlined paper.

Sammy wondered what the next catastrophe would be; then he tried to identify the final catastrophe. The apocalypse, he supposed, would probably involve peeing in his pants. He checked his vital signs: no, not yet, he didn't have to go. But he could still throw up, and the mere thought of it made it more likely. On the scale of offenses and mortifications, vomiting was less embarrassing than wetting oneself, but if he threw up now, here in Mr. Harding's classroom, it would never be forgotten, he thought, not as long as the school remained standing.

Kevin studied my message. He had straightened up, bringing a roseate cast to his cheeks—or at least the unbending appeared to be the cause of his glow. In our single, half-coherent, anxious, anguished phone conversation after the debacle, the last time we would ever speak, when in desperate fits and starts we tried to piece together what had happened, he told me that after he finished reading the note, he was surprised that Sammy was still there. He told the boy he could return to class.

Sammy had nearly reached the hallway when Kevin murmured, a new softness in his voice, "Son, wait a minute."

Sammy turned.

Kevin stood, contemplating the letter in hand, and he was seized by an impulse, and a different kind of smile, narrow and turned in on itself, was being forged around the ends of his mouth. "I need to write back."

Sammy entered the room again and the fifth graders responded with no less gusto or more kindness than they did the first time. Kevin sat behind his desk. He thought for a few moments, staring out the window into the playground and sports field as he gathered up the words he would use, before he began to pencil something at the bottom of the original note.

The boy waited in front of the class, fully exposed. Their exuberance for the moment depleted, the fifth graders fidgeted and muttered furiously. Focused on what he was writing, Kevin probably didn't notice, but every rustle and murmur, every chair squeak and snicker, ran through Sammy like a current. After each shock he waited for the next. Or, looking at it another way, he felt like a chicken on a barbecue spit. Or like a sheet of flypaper catching every indignity buzzing by his head. Kevin was taking long enough for me to come up with a long list of similes. Sammy was like an astronaut floating out of his capsule into a meteor swarm. Now he heard his name whispered, set free among the fifth graders. Someone was attempting to get his attention, rasping, "Sam-*my*! Sam-*my*!" The boy had to fight himself not to turn, and this struggle, evidently visible, only intensified the assault. Kevin didn't look up.

Sammy trained his eyes on the teacher, anxiously aware that a boy named George lurked in the periphery of his vision, at one of the desks in the first or second row. This George was a big kid, his proud bulk nearly rivaling an adult's. He walked with an adult's long strides. His voice had begun to change. He sweated freely. Standing together in the playground during recess, Kevin and I had seen him throw his weight around, facing down other fifth graders and even students from the middle school. George would occasionally occupy the top step of the slide, his butt barely accommodated, and block anyone else from using it. From that position he would survey the playground with the satisfaction of an emperor. With appropriate imperial grace, he would raise his hand and point at individual children who were running, throwing a ball, or skipping rope and announce which of them was a *homo*. "He is. He is. He isn't. He is. He's something else! He isn't." Whenever George issued these verdicts, Sammy would turn away, wherever he was in the schoolyard. Now George's proximity weighed on him like a thundercloud, or a malignancy.

Kevin took a long time to craft his response. The whispers turned into the roar of a cave-dwelling beast, yet the teacher remained at his desk in thought, his pencil suspended over the letter. Now Sammy was sure he would wet his pants. The urge was enormous. If he wasn't allowed to leave the room, everything would give way within seconds, everything representing much more than his bladder.

Kevin finally completed his reply, which, I gather, made my original note considerably less cryptic. He returned the sheet of paper to the manila envelope, folded the flap, pushed the clasp through the hole that obligingly presented itself, and pressed the clasp shut. His broad, square thumbs pushed hard against the device. He asked Sammy to return it to me.

The boy was chased from the room by one last bark of ridicule, contempt snapping at his heels. He rested in the hallway to collect himself near a row of stapled, multipage reports hung decoratively to showcase the class's work. The covers were drawn in colored pencil, more finely than anything that could have been done with a second grader's crayon. He tried to catch his breath. The need to urinate left him as suddenly as it had come. Instead perspiration prickled the sides of his body and the back of his scalp. His shirt was wet under the armpits. The envelope had returned to his hand, heavy with dampness and the burden of Kevin's response.

At first Sammy blamed himself for being sent on this errand. He had rushed through his penmanship exercises. If he had taken more time with them, as he was often told to do, someone else would have been sent. Another error: his life was composed of what even then seemed like a long series of errors. He had no idea what norms he had trespassed in Room 212. But he was also beginning to be aware that he was mostly guiltless for his improprieties. He was eight years old and couldn't be expected to know everything. His spirit was stricken and battered, weak and suppressed, yet somewhere buried within it, as if growing from a discarded seed, stirred a tiny sprout of something.

At the end of the hallway, having come up the stairs, a familiar figure gazed at the second grader: Dr. Fairmount. In the distant shadows that could not be penetrated by the glare of the fluorescents, gently swaying in the movement of the ether, he remained indistinct. He was more an idea of Dr. Fairmount than the man himself. As Sammy's own figure became clearer to him, the principal called his name. This may have been Dr. Fairmount's fourth or fifth correct guess of the day. He was really quite the phenomenon. "Out for a stroll?"

Sammy went to him and heard himself say hello, or something like it. Dr. Fairmount smiled down from a great height, stroking his chin as if he had a beard. His eyes found Sammy's. The boy couldn't look away.

"You must have skipped a few grades!"

Dr. Fairmount's presence filled the hallway. Sammy craned his neck to see his face, but he wasn't afraid. I don't think I would have been either. The principal's arrival was what was supposed to have happened.

"Here," the boy said.

The principal took the envelope from Sammy's hand, surprised. "This is for me?"

Sammy didn't reply.

Dr. Fairmount gingerly bent the clasp, which may already have suffered more stress than for which it had been designed. He extracted the page and turned it to catch the light. Ignoring the boy, he studied my message as fixedly as Kevin had. Sammy wondered if he had just made another grave mistake. Dr. Fairmount read Kevin's response. He looked up, gazing at the open door to the fifth-grade classroom down the hall, and then back at the boy. He re-animated his smile. He slid the correspondence into the envelope and pressed the clasp flat. The second or third time the envelope was opened again, at the end of the school day, in the principal's inner office, with the door shut, one of the wings of the clasp would snap off.

"I see," he now said blandly. "Thank you, you should go back to your class. Your teacher will be waiting for you."

Students weren't allowed to run in the halls, but Sammy nearly flew, relieved to have given Dr. Fairmount the envelope. The relief was evidence in itself that he had done the correct thing. He was down the stairs in just three perilous hops.

When he finally reached the safety of Room 112, I was handing out a new arithmetic worksheet. I stopped to ask him if he had found Mr. Harding. Still panting, Sammy nodded yes. I was pleased, and some small worry was extinguished. I went on with the lesson. At the same time, I was distracted by my efforts at telepathy, as I tried to guess what was passing through the mind of my friend directly above my head. I often thought I could hear the shuffle of his penny loafers or the tapping of chalk on his blackboard. I supposed that he had read the note, laughed or smiled, returned it to the envelope, and put it in a safe place.

Sammy was no more attentive now that he was back at his desk than he had been before I sent him upstairs. His face went loose, like an elderly man's. The light went out in his eyes. By some common but magical process, the major part of his being was returned to Mr. Harding's class, back to those sweaty-palmed three or five minutes. He was the subject of predatory whispers. He was drilled by unblinked stares. The fifth graders scorned him still.

Kevin kept his job. He had been at the school three years already. Dr. Fairmount and the parents liked him, and dismissing one of the fifth-grade teachers would have caused more trouble than it was worth. I presume, though, that Kevin was warned by the principal—firmly, but perhaps with compassion and a certain delicacy. As for the boy, Sammy, he could not have had any notion of the role he'd played in the arrival of a substitute teacher the very next day, followed by a permanent replacement two weeks later. He never wondered. Adults came into your life and left it for reasons of their own. Sammy would always consider the new person his one true second-grade teacher. By the time he graduated to the upper floor of the school, the circumstances of the day would have blurred into those related to other disasters. Sammy would never forget, however, the free-fall aloneness that he felt at the front of Mr. Harding's class, nor the fierce, bitter, knowing, and shaming percussions of an older child's laughter.

MR. IRAQ

Adam Zweig's mother couldn't have phoned at a worse time: he was on deadline—in fact, an hour past the drop-dead, absolute deadline for the magazine's cover story, the argument for single-payer, universal health care. Progressively frenzied editors had been calling his house all morning.

A senior writer at a small but influential political journal in 2005, the cold, dark-hearted year after the Bush-Kerry debacle, Adam had become convinced that the provision of decent medical treatment for every American was the crucial moral struggle of his generation. There was not a single domestic problem—entrenched poverty, racial division, outsourced labor—whose solution did not depend on reform of the medical industry. New substantive arguments had recently made themselves evident, accompanied by original rhetorical flourishes. The key device, of course, was to call the plan *universal health care*, as opposed to, say, *national medical program. Program* was too big-government; *medical* reminded people of illness; *national* would have evoked *nationalized*, which suggested *socialized* or, even worse, *socialised*. The argument required, as every argument did, a certain compositional nuance.

Now his mother had called.

Lillian shouted through the phone, "Your father's been arrested!"

Cold relief flooded Adam's veins, tingled his nerve endings, and opened his pores. His father was eighty-one. At that age, a baleful, morbid predicate could follow in any sentence in which *your father* was the subject. You felt as if you had dodged a bullet any time it didn't. Not that the past participle *arrested* didn't carry negative connotations. Still focused on a paragraph explaining how a rationalized medical-payment system would boost workers' productivity across the board, Adam struggled to comprehend.

"Wha—?"

"He was at the White House, protesting the war. They've locked up dozens of demonstrators. We need to go and post bail."

"He was arrested?"

"It has to be cash or credit and you have to sign him out. Otherwise they make him spend the night."

Adam's father had never before been arrested. No one in Adam's family, going back to great-grandfathers toiling in restive czarist provinces, had ever been arrested, to his knowledge. But none had ever been this old either. And this was old age for sure: his father's dignity, once as hard as a rock and just as unmoving and monumental, had recently stressed and fractured. He became easily muddled. A former lawyer, once silver of tongue and hair, a conspicuous, courtly presence in every room he entered, his father now lost his temper over small things, especially his recent inability, sometimes, to find the right word. In old age, against the demands of his failing body, you could see the flint of a man's character succumb to the elements: temperance, a flake; exactitude, a sliver; judgment, a crashing boulder whose absence was like a mountainside gash. Only in old age would his father do something as indecorous as get himself arrested.

"Ma, I'm writing an article. Max needed it two days ago. He's going to kill me."

"Your father's in jail! He doesn't have his medication!"

"The *printer's* waiting. That's how late I am."

"Adam!"

His father in jail: suddenly the image took on a fully dimensional vitality. There was no guarantee that the police had been solicitous of his age. Even an unresisted arrest could involve shoves and pushes, restraint positions, sharp-edged handcuffs. The jail could be drafty and damp. It almost certainly was. They could have put him in a cell with genuine lawbreakers.

"Okay, okay, give me a few minutes."

"No, come now. And pick me up first!" Lillian cried. Her hearing was perfect, but these days she always raised her voice over the phone. This was another development in his parents' passage through time. "I have his pills."

Adam scrolled up the essay, wondering if he could do anything for it within the next minute and a half. The piece was good, but still rough around the edges. Cody, the brilliant, underpaid copy editor about to be poached by a more prosperous publication, would fix some of the writing, and Adam would be able to make a few changes over the phone. He knew, though, that he hadn't delivered his point, hadn't quite ironcladded the argument: a reasonable person could still, damnably, disagree. This was so even though the article opened strongly and offered the prospect of setting the Democratic agenda for the next decade. In the miasmatic marshlands of defeat, seized by perplexity and grief that Bush could have been reelected when he had so blatantly mismanaged his first term, the Democrats needed an agenda.

Adam had expected that his story would get widespread attention—just before his contract with the magazine was up for renegotiation, which would coincide with that giddy moment when he would have to pay his son's first-semester tuition at Yale. Now it was only another opinion piece, one of dozens he had written in the last year that had left him vaguely dissatisfied. The pieces got done; Max was as happy as he allowed himself to get; Adam was making a living. Yet the great leviathan of American society moved on, absorbing his reasoned judgments—on immigration, on global warming, on a gun-safety compromise that would have settled the issue for all time—with the nonchalance of a woolly mammoth lumbering through a blizzard of Neolithic spears. This damned health-care piece was going to be just another chiseled rock tied to a stick.

His mother would be waiting for him in her driveway. He clicked the SEND button, took his cell phone, and hoped for the best. Disappointment tugged at him like an undertow.

By the time he reached Lillian, Adam was furious. "Why didn't he bring his medication?" he said as he left the car to open the door for her. "Why did he get himself arrested? Why did he even take part in this tiny, tiny, *tiny* demonstration that didn't even make the local news?" Adam demanded, waving at the car radio, which was tuned to the NPR station.

His mother's hands trembled as she closed the seat belt. A thin, small woman in a prim two-piece suit, she gazed through the windshield and murmured, "He's against the war."

"Does he really think this protest is going to save a single Iraqi or American life? Does he think protests and civil disobedience—" Adam stopped. "What did he do? Why did they arrest him? Please don't tell me he chained himself to the White House fence."

"He didn't," she said quietly. "The protesters had a permit, but they left their designated area when they thought they saw Bush's car. They wanted him to read their posters. They crossed a police line. But they only wanted him to read their posters."

"It was almost certainly not Bush's car. I don't think he's even back from Ottawa. Okay, let me rephrase the question. Do you think Dad would want to live in a country where vital foreign-policy issues are decided in response to street protests? Where presidents change direction because demonstrators rush their cars with posters?"

His mother remained composed. When not on the phone, her voice was tremulous and barely a whisper. "I don't know. You'll have to ask him yourself."

Adam was silenced. He headed the car downtown.

He and his father were not, technically, not speaking. They spoke over the phone several times a week, often about the weather, health issues involving his father's elderly friends, and, most gratifyingly, about the latest academic, literary, and musical laurels won by Adam's luminous teenage son, Jason, a rising cellist, who lived with his mother. Adam and Manny Zweig would even launch occasional conversational sallies, improbably enough, about the Redskins. But they never spoke about politics, which, for them, was tantamount to not speaking at all. And they took special care not to speak about the war.

They had once spoken about the war. They had spoken about it over the phone, in the car, and during intermissions at Jason's high school concert performances. They had spoken about it at every holiday dinner for a year, until Adam's cousins had put their hands over their ears and begged them to speak about partial-birth abortion instead. They had spoken about the war in epic head-to-head, toe-to-toe debates that had seemed endless and circular and always, it appeared, on the verge of being about something else, Adam wasn't sure what: Indolent adolescent summers? Former trashy girlfriends? Lamebrain career decisions? His divorce? No tables were thumped, no doors or phones had been slammed, and voices had hardly been raised, yet Lillian had often been near tears. This was, of course, before the war. Everything he had said at the time still echoed in his ears, like the sound of mortars. This is what he was fated to rehear: "Dad, whatever happens, after this war the Iraqi people will be better off." "*Dad*, just think for a moment what it would mean to have a functioning, prosperous liberal democracy in the Arab world." "*Dad!* I've seen the classified intel. I've spoken to people who know—I can't say who—but I can guarantee you that Saddam has WMD."

As a journalist deeply involved in current affairs, Adam Zweig had commanded an authority that his father, once a dominating voice on every political issue, could no longer pretend to. Adam regularly interviewed experts in the think tanks, left and right. He could cite unnamed sources in the Defense Department and even at the CIA. He had been to Afghanistan, with Enduring Freedom, on a white-knuckled, Pentagon-sponsored tour, snapping on body armor as his helicopter took evasive action over a Taliban stronghold.

He had returned home with vivid reports of what he saw, but Adam could communicate neither to his father nor his friends how, for him, something had changed. After two weeks in the company of battlefield officers and soldiers, he felt touched by their toughness and capability and their day-by-day nobility, so distant from his own days. They knew what they had to do; they were confident they could do it; they saluted crisply. At the Air Force base on the Diego Garcia atoll, waiting for his flight into Bagram, Adam had watched the bombers lift off for hours, mesmerized. Palms rustled in the distance, colossal, billowing thunderheads beyond them. A hermit crab scuttled across the tarmac. Gasoline fumes rose visibly like jinns from the lagoon's toxic waters. The jets' thunder rolled through him, right down to his bones, past his bones, right down to his DNA—the DNA that made him an American, contrary to any claims of ethnicity, history, culture, or politics. The officers he accompanied assumed that he was with them all the way.

There had been times when he had not been: Vietnam, of course, when Adam had protested the war on campus, but once again in more recent conflicts, when he had argued either against—or unenthusiastically in favor of, with numerous qualifications and sour observations—military action that in the end proved successful. Particularly after the first Gulf War, won so handily by America's superior weaponry and skillful diplomacy, he had found it fatiguing, even debilitating, to have been so deeply mistaken. He grew uncomfortable, at parties of friends, colleagues, and other nominally like-minded people, with the predictable, never-contradicted criticisms of American foreign policy muttered by—he would suddenly lift his head from his wine and look at them hard—smug, jeering, preening, theory-besotted, Euro-affected *assholes*. In the run-up to the new war against Saddam, he wanted to give his support to the military men and women he admired. He wanted to share in the pleasure of their inevitable victory.

At the magazine, which was still dispirited and unnerved by the 2000 election, Adam became the leading proponent of a militarily assertive foreign policy, even if it meant siding with the Republicans. There had been some in-house bloodletting, but Max, a renowned contrarian, had let Adam guide the magazine toward an early advocacy of the Iraq War, gaining beyond-the-Beltway prominence. Pride in his son's growing prestige had hardly tempered Manny's anger. He had canceled his subscription.

Now Adam's cell phone trilled. The copy editor, Cody, was calling.

"Hey."

"We need it!"

"It's sent. Check your in-box."

"Max is beside himself. If we don't make it to the printer's . . ."

Adam knew. The magazine had booked the time on the presses. There would be some ill-afforded penalties.

"It's there. It's done. Don't worry, it's wending its way through cyberspace even as we speak."

Adam glanced at the notepaper on which Lillian had written the specifics of his father's detention. The police had put the arrested protesters in a city maintenance garage in the Near Southeast, not far from the Navy Yard. Adam and Lillian approached it past some low industrial buildings. The garage was easy to find: a crowd was gathered in the street in front. Cops on horses stood by. Adam parked his car down the block.

The protest that began at the White House had evidently moved here, and Adam wondered if it was growing: at least two hundred people, mostly young, now furiously swarmed the locked entrance gate. They had thrown down their posters and were using their hands, feet, and mouths to erect a wall of noise against the police. "Let them go!" they shouted. "Let them go!" Some were in tears. A kid with his long, brown hair in a swollen hairnet sat cross-legged against a chain-link fence and pounded a bongo.

It was an ugly crowd, Adam thought. The kind of crowd that came out in small numbers to stand by the White House on a Monday morning would have to be dominated by the un- and underemployed, the frustrated and anguished, the blue-jeaned and bandannaed. His father. Visored, black-jacketed police stood in a line at the gate. In the street the mounted police loomed over the protesters, their horses stepping toward them, threatening to crush feet, keeping them hemmed in.

Lillian gripped Adam hard by the forearm.

They stood uncertainly at the assembly's seething periphery. Adam turned to a college-aged woman in a peasant blouse. "What's up?"

"Mass arrests," she said, nearly spitting. "Police brutality."

Now his mother's fingernails were digging into his arm. Adam forced their way to the head of the throng and found a reasonable-looking cop at the gate. Adam was wearing pressed chinos and a blue blazer and looked, if not like a lawyer, then at least like a law professor. He let Lillian, who was now vibrating with anxiety, explain that her eighty-one-year-old husband was inside. The cop was indeed reasonable. They were allowed into the garage's front office, where there were several city policemen and an officer in a parks uniform at a desk behind a Plexiglas window.

The bond process was both complicated and easy: attestations had to be made, oaths sworn, and identification documents produced, but then Adam handed over his credit card as if he were paying for lunch. The clamor outside had intensified, punctuated by bitter chants that filled the room but whose exact wording he couldn't distinguish. Manny Zweig was finally led through a doorway and into his son's custody.

He didn't look as if he had been beaten, but rather as if he had just struck someone else. His face was flushed, his jaw was set hard, and he glared directly ahead, ignoring the policeman who accompanied him. He didn't look at his family. A bead of sweat glistened across the top of his hairless head. He wore, not uncharacteristically, a gray business suit. In the last year or so, the suit had come to be a size too big.

"Dad, are you okay?"

He didn't respond.

Lillian said, "I have your pills."

"Outside," he grunted, breaking away from the cop.

Adam nodded to the impassive officer and mumbled a surreptitious "thank you." Respect for the workingmen who carried out the law, sometimes in difficult circumstances, had been one of the precepts with which Adam had been brought up. He and his mother followed Manny's long strides to the exit.

Adam's eyes closed in pain as he entered the sunlight. The crowd now seemed even more motley and restless. His father had stopped before the protesters, his arms raised in a victory salute. Their antiwar laments turned into cheers and then into a roar, followed by sustained, raucous applause, the crowd acknowledging their comrade's freedom and his advanced age. Adam and Lillian stayed back, allowing Manny to accept the recognition on his own. They had done this before: at lectures, at banquets, at law-firm dinners. Although he disapproved of his father's participation in the protest, Adam felt a familiar electric twinge of pride; also a distant, shameful, familiar shudder of resentment.

As they entered the crowd, individual protesters came over, took Manny Zweig's hand, and thanked him for standing fast against the police state. He turned with them to face the building, joining in their rage at the arrests.

"It's a travesty," he said. "Suppression of the right of assembly. Suppression of the right to dissent."

Adam said weakly, "We should go . . ."

Lillian tugged on Manny's arm, but his brown wingtips remained planted where they were.

Adam's phone went off in his inside jacket pocket.

Cody said, "I still don't have it!"

"Yahoo!" Adam groaned, in explanation. He stepped away from his mother and father. "Give it another minute."

"I *did* get an e-mail from you, but it was a blank screen. There was no attachment."

Adam felt as if he had just smashed his head against an open door. "Shit, shit, shit! I attached the story," he protested, but even as he made his defense, he desperately failed to locate a memory of performing the procedure. He would have had to go to another screen and typed in the file name. He clearly recalled clicking SEND, but that was all.

"Please, send it again! Max is on the phone with the printer's right now."

"Sure, sure," Adam said, mortified at the thought of the empty, attachmentless e-mail. "I just have to get back home."

"Adam, where *are* you? What's *that*?"

" 'No justice, no peace.' But I'll be home in three minutes," he promised, knowing he couldn't get to his machine for at least another half hour.

He went back to his parents. His father was still glowering at the police, and even at their horses. Adam said, "Listen, I have an urgent work situation. I've got to get home right now. I need something on my computer."

Manny took Lillian by the arm. "Go," he told Adam. "We'll get home on our own."

"You're blocks from the Metro and you'll never find a cab here. Just come. I have to stop at my house, send my piece, and then I'll take you home."

"The car's parked at G and Eighteenth."

Adam threw up his hands. "You drove in? Parking *and* bail? You owe me one hundred and thirty dollars, by the way. And you have a court date June sixth. You better show."

"Don't worry, I'll show. Those bastards will be sorry."

"I bet." Adam was virtually pushing his parents forward, moving in a stream of other departing protesters. They had stopped singing and had sullenly abandoned their posters. Their point had been made, but the war went on, and would be going on, as it was today, a year from today, and the year after that. Two thousand and five would eventually prove to be early in the war. Still brooding about the article imprisoned on his hard drive, Adam wanted only to get to his car. What a numskull he was. Max would be furious for weeks. Fortunately, the car was just on the next block and there'd be no traffic this time of day. He could leave his parents in the car while he ran into the house. The mission: attach the file, send it to Cody, call Max, and make profuse, preemptive apologies. Then hit him right away with a story idea for the next issue. Change the subject with something provocative: Massive federal investment for early childhood education?

Adam turned to encourage his parents to keep up and realized that someone had been looking at him. It was a young man in his twenties, a tall guy in a black T-shirt that read IMPEACH AMERICA. His chin was spotted by a scraggly, reddish-brown soul patch that matched an impressive tangle of hair on his head. The guy continued to stare, a knowing cast to his face.

He finally declared, "I saw you on *Meet the Press*."

"No, you didn't," Adam replied, trying to brush past. He could see his car. He took out his keys. The guy kept pace with him, still studying his features. He wasn't satisfied. Adam couldn't help himself. He said, "It was *This Week with George Stephanopoulos*, probably."

"I remember now. You're Alan Zweig. You write for some magazine."

"Adam. We're in a bit of a hurry." He indicated his parents, who lagged a few steps behind. Lillian wasn't as quick as she used to be.

The young man held his ground. "You were so strident about the war. You promised an easy victory. You said defeating Saddam was the vital challenge of our time. You compared Iraq to Rwanda, you compared it to Nazi Germany, you said no intellectually honest progressive could possibly oppose the war. You said it was racist to believe that the Iraqis wouldn't embrace a pluralistic democracy. You wrote op-ed articles. I saw you all over TV that winter! You were like a total front man for Bush and Cheney."

"That's right," Manny cried, hoarse with anger. "He was Mr. Iraq."

"Dad!"

The youth recalled, "Yeah, and that was you with George Stephanopoulos. You were livid at the antiwar movement. Your face went dark. You nearly got out of your seat. You said we were living in a September tenth world. That was a crock, another fraudulent attempt to link Saddam to 9/11."

Adam stepped around the youth and reached the car. As he halted there, several other protesters stopped too, drawn to the argument. Some had heard enough to murmur their assent.

Adam shook his head slowly, trying to show patience. "No, what I meant by that was that the war's opponents didn't accept the realities of asymmetrical warfare. The lesson of 9/11, for those of us paying attention, is that minor powers and small terrorist cells now have equal means to inflict enormous strategic losses."

"He's doing it again!" Manny yelled, stamping his feet. Lillian gasped and made a little whimpering cry. The stranger seemed frightened, perhaps of a medical emergency, and took two steps back. Adam reached out to catch his father if he fell. Manny said, "He's doing it again! He's trying to conflate Saddam and Al Qaeda! The biggest damned catastrophe in the history of American foreign policy, and he's still defending it! With lies!"

The dozen young men and women standing by were stunned into silence. They rotated toward Adam, surrounding him with their beards and piercings, their posters and imprecatory T-shirts, and waited for his response.

Adam clicked open the car locks and pulled open the front passenger door. "Listen," he said. "I'd love to take more shit from everyone, but I have to go."

"You're running!" asserted the young man with the soul patch. "You're cutting and running."

"I'm not running. Dad, Mom, please get in the car. Please! Now!"

Adam took his father by his sinewy right arm. Manny Zweig glared, but allowed his son to help him into his seat. Adam placed Lillian in the back. As a reporter, he had braved rioters in Panama, stone-throwers in Gaza, free-firing Russian troops in Chechnya, hard-assed ATF goons in Texas, and rampaging paramilitaries in the Congo, but his mother hadn't. Her face was the color of ashes.

"Cut and run!" one of the protesters called out. She was seconded by another: "Yeah, cut and run!" The protesters, whose numbers around the car were growing, hooted and shouted derisively, "Cut and run! Cut and run! Cut and run!" The bongo player punctuated each beat, joined by rhythmic clapping. "Cut and run!"

Adam went around to the driver's side, trying to ignore the chants. Inside the car they seemed even louder. The drumming reverberated through the roof. He jerked the car out into traffic, followed by applause and war whoops.

He sped down M Street, dodging slower-moving vehicles. He considered taking the 14th Street Bridge. He could probably shave off a minute or two there.

Without looking at his father, he growled, "Thanks for your support."

His father mumbled, not quite under his breath, "Cut and run."

Adam drove hard, the protesters' catcalls still bouncing around the interior of the car. His face was red, he knew. His armpits weeped. He was enraged: by the protesters' mob behavior, by their reductionist arguments, by his father. But it wasn't only anger that made him hot. The war *was* catastrophic. It had cost the lives and limbs of thousands of Americans. It had destroyed the lives of good Iraqi men, women, and children. It had destabilized the region. It had empowered Iran. It had empowered reactionary elements in American politics. Something oncogenic had been switched on, and now that thing was running wild through the organism. He knew the particulars better than those people in the street did. He tried not to dwell on the particulars. He had to rehearse his early-childhood-education pitch to Max. His parents were silent, trying to bridle their own galloping thoughts about the confrontation, but as the car crossed the Potomac, their inner monologues were stilled one by one, as each of them realized that a familiar voice was speaking over the radio, a voice they each knew intimately.

The theme this afternoon on the NPR call-in show *Talk of the Nation* was the American military. Earlier in the program some troops had telephoned from Iraq, and while he was parking the car, Adam had distractedly heard a single soldier's nightmare story: his patrol had struck an IED in Marwaniyah, in Anbar Province. The man next to him was cut in two. Blind with panic, rage, and grief, the troops fired antitank weapons at the closest home. It went up in flames. Then they fled. The soldier later learned only civilians were inside, including children, inevitably, and he was bewildered by what he and his comrades had done, and specifically by the chain of events that had brought them to that place to do it. The stateside callers who responded were sympathetic, many blaming the administration for starting an unwinnable war. Adam hadn't been paying attention. He hadn't heard the current caller identify himself or begin his comments, but now he listened intently.

". . . went to war with too few troops," the caller was saying. "That's indisputable. Whether we were for the war or opposed it, we have to recognize that without more boots on the ground we can't win or even prevent a ruinous defeat—a defeat that will decisively undermine national security. How will we get these new soldiers? Bribe more low-income Americans into serving? Pay off more private contractors to act as mercenaries? Pressure more small, weak East European and third-world countries to supply more troops? The most honest, most moral, most democratic, course would be to activate the draft. Make it efficient, make it fair, just take what you need—but we have to activate the draft."

Lillian gasped. "It's him!"

The voice on the radio was reedy and breathy, its sober intellectuality distinctly flavored by a soft, rising Georgia lilt inherited from Adam's ex-wife. The caller was immediately identifiable. It was Adam's son, Jason.

The NPR host asked, "Caller, do you believe there's sufficient public support for a draft?"

"Not now there isn't. The Republicans haven't asked for national sacrifice and neither have the Democrats. It's a disgrace. This is the reason why some friends and I at Fairfax High School"—that was, in fact, Jason's school—"have begun a petition drive, in favor of a draft. We have three hundred signatures so far, and we're making contact with people at other schools all over the country."

Manny demanded, "Did you know about this?"

"No," Adam said darkly.

The host observed, "Not a single prominent politician has come out in favor of a draft. It sounds like a nonstarter."

"Lynn, I recognize that," Jason said. "I know it's unlikely we'll get a draft anytime soon. But if they were listening to today's show, especially to Sergeant Gallagher's call from Marwaniyah, I think our leaders would realize the practical and moral necessity. For several difficult weeks now, I've been moving toward a decision. Lynn, Sergeant Gallagher has helped me make that decision. I can't stand by while men like him are risking everything in Iraq. There's a U.S. Army recruiting office in the mall over here in Fairfax. It's open until six. After this call, I'm going to drive there and enlist. It's the least I can do for my country."

Lillian's hand flew to her chest. "Oh my God! Oh my God!"

Adam said, "Bullshit."

"Caller . . .," the NPR host began tentatively, unsettled by Jason's declaration. She paused for several moments of dead air. You could hear Jason's breathing over the line. "That's quite a decision. I wish you the best of luck with your . . . service. Thank you for your call. This is *Talk of the Nation*. The lines are open."

There was silence in the car. Adam changed lanes, for no reason, then went back to his original lane.

"This is terrible," Manny whispered, for a moment not angry. "He's going to enlist. This is awful. Look what we've done!"

Adam said, "He's not going to enlist."

"How do you know?"

"He got a 730 in math, 750 in his verbals, and 790 in critical reasoning. He wouldn't last two weeks in *sleepaway camp*. He knows I listen to this show. He's just yanking my chain."

"You always think you have the answers," Manny accused furiously. "About Iraq, about Iran, about Bush, about the entire course of human history. He could be on his way to the recruiting office right now! Once he signs the papers, they've got him."

Lillian moaned.

Adam said, "Don't you think I know my own son?"

"Don't you think you can ever be wrong?" Manny asked. "And don't you think that being wrong can have consequences? If not for you, then for other people?"

Adam scowled, but took his phone from his blazer and handed it to his father. "Of course I do," Adam muttered, the words ascending from his guts and through his mouth and lips as rough and alkaline as road gravel. "Call him, you'll see."

Manny opened the phone, but before he could touch the keypad, Adam grabbed it back. "No, I'll call him, that little twerp." He punched the speed dial.

Jason answered on the first ring.

Adam said, "Nice stunt."

"It wasn't a stunt. I was serious about the draft. Don't forget, I told you the war was going to be a disaster. Now we probably need another hundred thousand troops over there, and a draft is the most progressive, honorable method of getting them. I was just being logical, trying to advance the argument. It was not a stunt."

Adam turned to his parents. "It was a stunt. He's not joining the Army."

Jason protested, "I could!"

"I'll send you a salami."

"What?"

"You nearly gave your grandparents heart attacks. I have them in the car with me. Pops just got himself arrested at a peace demonstration."

Jason made a low whistle. "No way. Let me talk to him."

But another call was coming in. Adam looked at the display. He told his son he'd call him back.

"Max, I'm pulling into my driveway right now. Stand by, I'll have it for you in a minute."

There was a heavy preliminary rumble over the line, like water in a heating kettle. Something was rising and gathering force: a voice. It was moist, it was kinetic, it was contained under pressure, barely.

"We missed the print run," the voice finally intoned.

"Shit, I'm sorry. It's my fault."

"We missed the print run," Max repeated. "That cost us. Then we had to reschedule—for Wednesday. That's two days, and because the distributor missed the pickup, it won't go out until Thursday. That means readers will have the magazine in their hands for three fewer days before the next issue. That means they lose three days' exposure to our ads. Our advertisers will demand a discount."

Adam was stopped at a light, only a mile and a half from his house. No other traffic was in the intersection or approached it. He considered Jason's argument about the draft. It was sound, consistent with liberal principles. Abolishing the draft had been a Nixon-era mistake, freeing presidents from the political costs of war. There was no petition, of course, but perhaps Adam could encourage his son to turn his thoughts into an op-ed. Adam inched forward, but the light remained resolutely red.

He said to Max, "We have advertisers?"

Max was silent, except for the cacophony of sighing, grunting, breathing, and percolating that was his lugubrious self at rest.

Adam promised, "I'll send you the piece now. Actually, since the print run's pushed back, if I can work on it another day—"

When Max replied, speaking slowly, the rumble was opened to full throttle. "Forget it, Adam."

"Okay, okay, I'll e-mail it now."

"I said forget it."

The traffic signal turned and Adam sped off. He was suddenly aware of the dull, aching pressure of the cell phone against his temple. He pulled the phone away for a moment. The side of his face was wet.

He said, "Don't be an idiot. It's the most important story you'll publish this year, the manifesto for a single-payer, easy-to-access universal health program that will give the Democratic Party real purpose. Every potential candidate will read this. It's going to be debated on the Sunday talk shows. Years from now we'll look back at this time as the moment when we became serious about providing every American with decent medical care. Medical care is the key to eradicating systemic poverty and American wage decline. It's vital to building a humane, progressive society. This is exactly what the magazine should be in front of. How can you forget it?"

"We'll pay you a kill fee."

"A *kill fee*? After what I've done for this magazine? Max, please, that's an insult."

"You think? Try this then: go fuck yourself, Adam."

As Adam closed the cell phone, he realized that his father was staring. Disapprovingly, of course. He had heard both sides of the conversation. This was not, Adam supposed, the way lawyers in Manny's firm had conducted business. Adam checked the rearview mirror. Lillian was shocked, again.

He said, "Max has been under a lot of stress."

There were many other current-affairs publications, of course, publications Adam had already written for and others whose editors had sought his work. There were better, more widely read magazines. He could easily redo the health-care piece for one of them. They'd be pleased to have it, and then he would explore a new contractual relationship, perhaps something more lucrative.

Adam and his parents had almost reached his house, but he realized that nothing any longer urgently needed to be e-mailed. He told them he would take them back to their car. He made a quick left onto the next street and, carelessly accelerating, hit a speed bump that had been lying in wait. His mother voiced a small shriek. The car bounced, and for a brief moment the front of its chassis lifted up, and all Adam could see before him was a void of blue sky.

The car gently returned to earth and he made another left and returned in the direction of the city. But with the Capitol neatly framed in his windshield, Adam could think only of that emptiness he had just glimpsed, its cleanliness and honesty and purity. He felt that he was traveling on a ballistic trajectory toward it or through it. The sensation was as if he were still airborne, up above. But what exactly was he above? He was above something. And the thought that came to him at that moment, the District laid out below him and the federal monuments staring him in the face, was that he had somehow cleared the loftiest spires of American politics.

He didn't need to write about politics, did he? Nor did he have to write for a disposable magazine, on disposable issues. A literary agent had once intimated that some decent advances were to be had by an established journalist such as himself. The book wouldn't need to be about politics at all. Damn, not at all, he thought. He could, for example, do a book about a set of high school baseball prospects from some small towns and suburbs, representative in their diversity, as they embarked on their arduous ascents to the majors. What were the pressures? How did their pursuit keep them apart from the general run of humanity? How did their stories reveal the basic contradictions inherent within the idea of professional sports? Adam also recalled recently meeting a NASA scientist who told him that astronomers would shortly be capable of detecting life on other worlds. New extrasolar planets were being detected every week. Gigantic radio telescopes roamed the skies hoping to be struck by a bolt of intelligence. No story this century would be more important than the discovery of extraterrestrial life.

These ideas and others that wildly rushed into his thoughts unbidden left Adam trembling with anticipation. In his hands and the typing fingers that lightly gripped the steering wheel, he felt throb the big ideas that would change minds, the incipient arguments to be incarnated by language, and the potent words and sentences that would transport him to landscapes far, far, far, illimitably far, from the dire, sun-blistered streets of Marwaniyah.

SHVARTZER

The old man had received a disturbing call from New York the night before, from the son of his best friend. Donald said he had just spoken to his father, who had rambled on bitterly for twenty minutes and then hung up without saying goodbye. He had railed about the cleaning girl, an unlocked laundry-room door, the condo board, and things that made no sense at all. Without thinking, Mr. Robinson assured him that his father was fine, that he had always been a bit of a grouch.

But now Mr. Robinson wished he hadn't spoken so quickly—an eighty-year-old habit he was still trying to overcome. His friend Mr. Brown had indeed been very confused in recent weeks. The other day he had wandered over to the next block of three-story condos as white as desert-bleached bone and mistaken the first of the buildings for his own. He had tried to enter the corresponding apartment, even though its door was a different color. His key wouldn't fit. Thrashing the door with his fist, the physical strength that had been the pride of his youth hardly diminished, Mr. Brown had shouted, "You'll never evict me, never! Never, you fucking fuckers!" The people inside were frightened enough to call Security. In the last few months Mr. Brown's fury at the world of ever-younger people had consumed him. Even after his error was explained, he continued to swear at the quivering inhabitants, a just-retired couple from Parkchester. The poster in their front window promoted Ed Koch for mayor in the coming election.

Mr. Robinson didn't want to admit that Mr. Brown was slipping. The wrong word could convince Donald to put his friend in a nursing home, the last turn of the last lap. But what if something was seriously wrong? It was becoming clear that Mr. Brown was no longer taking care of himself. When Mr. Robinson found him by the pool this morning, he was wearing the same perspiration-stained, long-sleeved, button-down shirt that he had worn all week. Mr. Robinson believed Mr. Brown had given up washing his clothes, apparently a boycott of the laundry room. And neighbors had complained about odors from his apartment, which he had dismissed with insults and threats. Mr. Brown wouldn't allow anyone in, not even to remove the garbage. If someone didn't take action soon, the condo board would intervene.

A few women young enough to be the men's daughters—but no younger—sat at the pool's edge. The water sliced their stout, marbled legs at the knees. Mr. Robinson nodded hello, and one or two smiled back, maybe flirtatiously. He recognized them as the women who had first raised the alarm about the unlocked laundry rooms. There had been an incident in a laundry room in another community, in Pompano Beach. Everyone was talking about it.

Mr. Brown occupied a lounge chair in the direct sun, perspiring in his long gray trousers and black shoes. He had never, Mr. Robinson thought, quite accepted the idea of Florida. In the past seven years Mr. Brown's only concession to the place was a crumpled straw hat, the kind of hat tourists buy.

"It's like Russia," Mr. Brown said, instead of good morning. He was not referring to Florida. "The anti-Semitism. The violence. The gangs. You see them coming, you cross the street. And even then you're not safe. They can cross the street too, you know. You can't go into certain neighborhoods anymore or walk certain streets in your own neighborhood. Hah, a free country. It's like a slow-motion pogrom that never ends, year in and year out."

Mr. Robinson dragged over a chair. "Abe, there's no comparison. They killed thousands of Jews in the pogroms."

"They're not killing Jews now? Don't you read the paper?" Mr. Brown asked, his face splotching crimson. "All over the city. Brownsville. Pitkin Avenue. Flatbush Avenue. Howard Beach. Look at my grandson. They knocked out his teeth for a pair of sneakers."

Mr. Robinson grimaced. He knew the story, of course. No one in the condo community didn't. Only three months earlier, Mr. Brown's seventeen-year-old grandson, Nicky, had been mugged a block from his home in Riverdale. The muggers had put the barrel of a revolver in his mouth and their hands in his pockets. When all they found was small change, they removed the gun and beat his face with it. As further consolation for not finding any money, they took his sneakers, a pair of black high-tops.

"Terrible," Mr. Robinson murmured, for perhaps the hundredth time. He regretted his impatience with the story. Nicky was a sweet boy and what had happened to him was truly awful. He repeated, "Terrible. But listen, I have to tell you the truth, Abe, I'm worried. I know you'd tell me if you were worried, so now I have to tell you I'm worried. This is what I'm worried about: the sanitary conditions around your apartment. The neighbors are going to the board and, you know, they have the right."

"Fuck 'em. Fordham Road," Mr. Brown declared. "Now, that was a high-class place. The finest people in the Bronx shopped there, doctors and lawyers. And the streets were *clean*—you wouldn't think to throw a paper on the sidewalk any more than you'd throw down a dollar bill. But look at it now. If a Jew wanted to walk down Fordham Road, they'd murder him."

Mr. Robinson was about to object that it wasn't only Jews who were threatened; no whites would feel safe in those neighborhoods, and in fact any outsiders were likely to feel uncomfortable, whatever the color of their skin, though he knew this argument wouldn't placate Mr. Brown, and perhaps the last part of the statement wasn't true. Something had in fact happened in New York in the three decades since the war. The city that had been the best home for the Jews in the history of the world had gradually become as inimical to them as nearly everywhere else. Jews had lived safely in modest, tight-knit enclaves for years, mostly in harmony with neighbors of other ethnicities. Now in the schools gangs preyed on Jewish kids *and* Jewish teachers, and on the streets the Jews faced harassment and taunts. Newspapers reported daily muggings and assaults. So the Jews would leave: after all, for Mr. Robinson and Mr. Brown's generation, every life was a biography of flight, from ancestral homes in Europe, then to one shaky, temporary refuge after another, and then to America. The lesson of the twentieth century was that you *should* leave; it was foolish to overstay your welcome. In the Jews' former neighborhoods, only the businesses they owned remained, and those businesses soon dwindled away too, leaving, in many cases, empty, unrentable storefronts, or marginal enterprises geared to the poor: check-cashing places, barbecue joints, barbershops, incense and bead shops, and cult churches. People would say the neighborhood had "changed over," as if it were as natural as the turning of the leaves in the fall, and just as fatal.

"Look at East Tremont Avenue," Mr. Brown said. "A neighborhood full of honest working people, nobody had to lock their doors, you could go out at night. And what happened? They turned it into a slum. Sixteen-year-old girls pushing three-hundred-dollar strollers to the welfare office! And remember when Miami was a classy place? They wouldn't let them over the bridge, except for the help. You can't live there now, and you can't trust the help anywhere." He nodded in the direction of a passing, white-shirted attendant. The community employed dozens of them. "And even in Riverdale, with its fancy homes, they mug my grandson. A straight-A student, a serious, nice boy." He spat. "Bastards."

Mr. Robinson recalled the grandson; he had come to Florida with his parents last year. He was a slight boy with a soft, creamy complexion so far untouched by a razor. His jet-black hair tousled nearly down to his shoulders. Appreciating their reprieve from the New York winter, his parents treaded water in the condo pool, but Nicky preferred to sit on a chaise in cutoff jeans with his nose in a book. His parents never admonished him to use the pool; they were apparently proud of his bookishness.

Nicky's parents invited Mr. Robinson to come with them to a restaurant in Boca Raton. On the way there, in the backseat of the car, the book open in his lap, Nicky had stared at the broken shanties that lined the side of Highway 441 for miles. It was the main north-south thoroughfare, laid down at the edge of the vast Loxahatchee wetlands. Wash hung on clotheslines, but the clothes were faded and ragged, and he may have thought that the board and cinder-block structures were abandoned. Windows were cracked or missing; the door of one shack hung open, falling off its hinges. In front of the place was a little garden of auto parts, soaking in the sun in puddles of motor oil. As their car stopped at a traffic light, a young, very dark-skinned man suddenly appeared in the doorway and looked at them, the whites of his eyes as bright as anything in the Florida landscape. His overalls were half-unbuttoned. Nicky's mother was embarrassed when her son stared back. She said you made it worse by staring. She turned away, but Mr. Brown had teased the boy, "You see the *shvartzer*? Don't worry about him. He's got color TV inside."

Now Mr. Robinson said, "Please, Abe, don't make yourself crazy. You're right one hundred percent. But we have to talk turkey. You have a contract with the condo board. If you don't keep your place up to certain standards, they can sue."

"Let 'em. Sons of bitches. They should do something about locking the laundry room before they start with me. I'll countersue. Don't think I won't."

"C'mon, Abe. Do you need the aggravation?" Mr. Robinson said, shaking his head sadly. "Why can't you clean a little? Why should you live in *filth*? You had a girl. What happened to her?"

"I fired her. She was a thief. She took something every time: a hat, a pair of gloves, my wristwatch. My good cuff links are gone! She thought I wouldn't miss them. But I'm old, not blind."

"We can get you another girl. My girl is very good, a real sweetheart."

Mr. Brown scowled. When the scowl vanished, his face hardened and his eyes cleared and narrowed. Decades vanished. Mr. Robinson recognized the man who had fought, sometimes with his fists, to make a life for himself and his family in New York. The former owner of a small construction company, a defier of mobs and unions, a man who could carry his own bags of cement past the pickets, Mr. Brown had never stopped fighting.

He declared, "They have to be watched every minute. First thing she did when she came in was to open the windows. She told me, 'A woman's got to breathe.' I said, 'Nigger, I know what you're doing.' That's right, I called her nigger. Do you think they don't call you worse? She acted as if she didn't hear me. She pretended to lock the windows when she left, but I found one that wasn't locked, for her boyfriend to come back and rob me."

"Abe, I've seen your cleaning girl. She must be sixty years old. I think her boyfriend days are over."

"The bastard was going to rob me. Even kill me. But he couldn't do it. He couldn't even find my apartment. He was drunk or he was on drugs. He fell asleep! Hah!"

Mr. Robinson raised his hand to wave away the story. "Now I think we can both go upstairs and straighten a little. We can take out the garbage, do the dishes, open the windows, maybe ease the situation, if you know what I mean."

"Not necessary," Mr. Brown muttered.

"If it's not going to be us, it's going to be the condo board. They'll do it themselves."

"Good. I'll take them to court for trespassing."

Mr. Brown leaned from the edge of his lounge chair, his rheumy eyes bulging. This was not how Mr. Robinson had wanted the conversation to go.

"You'll take them to court!" he said, forcing a sarcastic laugh. He grinned and looked around the pool, as if for someone with whom to share this. The women at the edge of the pool ignored them. "What a greener."

"I'm a citizen fifty years."

"Citizen of *what*?" Mr. Robinson said with extravagant disdain. "Citizen of the Bronx. Citizen of East Tremont Avenue. But this is Florida. This is redneck country. They're not going to be interested in looking at your citizenship papers. This is where you can get a ticket for having New York plates."

Driving down last year, Mr. Brown's son Donald had been pulled over in South Carolina and then again just south of Jacksonville.

"I'll get a lawyer. He'll take care of it."

Mr. Robinson laughed and ruefully shook his head. "You know, Abe, you don't understand the situation. The condo board runs this place, they're the law of the land. You don't have rights here. You can't complain if they come up to your room and go through your personal possessions. They'll throw out what they feel like throwing out. Wake up, Abe. Remember, you're a Jew in the South. You're lucky they let you live here."

"You're nuts. This is my country," Mr. Brown said, but Mr. Robinson caught the waver in his voice.

"Now, let's go and fix up your apartment a little bit," he said, pulling himself up from his chair. "C'mon, it'll take fifteen minutes."

"It'll be a test case," Mr. Brown growled, but he too, very slowly, lifted himself to a standing position.

Mr. Robinson didn't acknowledge his triumph. Mr. Brown may have been a fighter; his friend had played poker. They climbed the staircase that ran up the outside of Mr. Brown's building, both of them resting every few steps. At each pause, Mr. Brown muttered oaths at the condo board.

They reached his floor.

"That's where I found him," Mr. Brown said, waving at the laundry room.

"Who?"

"The *shvartzer.*"

"What *shvartzer*?"

"You know, the *shvartzer.*"

At the door to his apartment, Mr. Brown's spotted, shaking hands labored to work the key. Finally, they turned the lock, and Mr. Robinson realized that the neighbors were lucky Mr. Brown never raised his windows. The stink rolled out the open door like a fog. Inside the deeply shadowed apartment filthy dishes were piled in the kitchen and laundry was scattered on the floor.

"Abe, is there something going bad in the fridge? Do you have problems with your toilet?" he asked, choking, his hand up to his face. "You know, we pay maintenance. They'll send over a plumber."

But the worst smell wasn't coming from the bathroom.

Mr. Robinson stopped in the hallway. "Are you putting garbage in your closet?"

"Yeah. That's where I hid it."

"Well, you can't do that." Mr. Robinson's head spun.

"Garbage, that's right," Mr. Brown said angrily. "You want to see my garbage?"

"Yes. No."

"It was the middle of the night and I couldn't sleep, thinking about Nicky, what they did to him. They knocked out his teeth for a pair of sneakers! I got out of bed and took my flashlight. I went out to see if anyone was in the laundry room. And the *shvartzer* was there, lying next to the dryer. A good, heavy flashlight I have. The girl comes the next Wednesday and she doesn't say nothing. She doesn't say, 'Where's my boy?' She doesn't say, 'Since I left the window unlocked, weren't you robbed?' She acts like always. I say, 'So where's your boyfriend?' And she says, 'What boyfriend? I thought you were my boyfriend.' And I say, 'Get out, you black bastard, get out, you black bastard, get out, you black bastard. I'll call Security. I'll call the police.' She says she'll never come back. 'Good,' I say, 'you're fired!' "

Mr. Robinson mumbled, "Oh my God," as the closet door swung open, and even though he would live another sixteen months, he would never be the same. He would repeat the story many hundreds of times.

His friend Mr. Brown would not enjoy the same opportunity more than once or twice. His native strength would desert him abruptly, completely, and catastrophically within twenty-four hours, a world-cleaving stroke that withdrew him from the custody of the Palm Beach County Sheriff's Office.

For the rest of his life, Mr. Robinson would describe the stench of the apartment and what he saw there to policemen, social workers, nursing-home attendants, and whoever else would either listen or pretend to listen. What he didn't tell them, because he didn't know why he should keep recalling it, was about the time before all this happened, that afternoon a year earlier when Donald had taken them to the restaurant in Boca Raton, a big "New York–style" delicatessen with pickles in a chrome bucket at every table.

Nicky had taken just two small bites from his pastrami sandwich, and while the adults talked, he stared into his plate. He had not said anything in the car and he had not looked at his book. Mr. Robinson and his parents made no sign that they noticed, but the boy's grandfather saw it all. The sandwich lay there. Without warning, but with his left hand clenched in a fist, Mr. Brown reached across the table with his right, grabbed Nicky's sandwich, and began eating it himself, tearing at the meat with his entire mouth, swallowing it before it was even chewed, even though his own sandwich was only half finished. Nicky had burst into tears.

LASER

The fifteen hundred milliwatts delivered to his right eye felt exactly as Michael Nash had expected them to, an insistent, penetrating tickle, and he was unsure, while he was experiencing the procedure, whether he would characterize it as painful but not unpleasant, or unpleasant but not painful. The lightning strike lasted about a second and a half, Dr. Jaeger paused, and then he reissued the charge, to another section of the eye's anatomy. This time as the flare died away there was a lingering burn. Jaeger breathed hard as he shifted his position in the chair on the other side of the machine, emphasizing to Nash the moment's intimacy. He could see the glaucoma specialist as a softly defined, translucent figure beyond the probe. Nash never flinched. He remained with his eye nestled in the apparatus's rubber socket, a good patient, attentive to the doctor's instructions.

When it was over, a nurse placed a patch over his eye and led him to a chair in the corridor. Demonstrating his fortitude, Nash tried to use his untreated eye to read something in *Scientific American*, but he was too fatigued and distracted. He had actually seen the laser bolt twisting across his field of vision. The light had illuminated the inside of his eye, a vast, wet jungle landscape distinguished by viny flora and darting tubular insects. After an hour Jaeger examined the eye and pronounced himself satisfied. Nash's wife, Kara, arrived and brought him home for some mandated bed rest. While he lay among his electronic devices, she served him soup, because that seemed like the thing to have after an operation, even a minor one. She tenderly removed his eye patch that evening. She expressed sympathy for his glaucoma, but she was also indulgently amused, as if the procedure were another of Nash's science projects, like his rooftop weather station, his beer-making apparatus, and his telescope-lens-grinding kit. She looked for a brief moment at his eye and announced, "It's still there."

Within a day Nash was ready to leave the bed. Jaeger had predicted that the vision in his right eye would remain blurred for several days or a couple of weeks, but he experienced no pain. By Monday, even though his vision had hardly cleared, Nash felt well enough to drive. He was impatient to return to school and looked forward to sharing the details of the operation with his sixth-period eleventh-grade physics class, his favorite that year. He drove anxiously alert, the radio off, with his right eye shut most of the way.

The class had covered light and laser technology a few months earlier, so Nash was justified in presenting a lesson about the procedure. The students crowded to the front of the class to better see the large poster diagram of the eye. The interior of the eye, Nash explained, was filled with a transparent liquid that maintained the organ's proper shape. With glaucoma, he said, the intraocular pressure rose above normal, damaging the retinal nerve tissue at the back of the eye and limiting its field of receptivity to light. Drugs were usually the first treatment for the condition. In conventional surgery—he wrote *trabeculectomy* on the board; someone wanted to know if it would be on the test—a tiny part of the eye's surface was removed to create a vent that allowed some of the fluid to escape. Argon laser surgery, *trabeculoplasty*, was a much less invasive and comparably effective alternative. He passed around a picture of the laser apparatus that he had photocopied from a magazine in Jaeger's office.

One of the presumed stoners said, "Doesn't marijuana work, Mr. Nash? Haven't they found that weed lowers the pressure?"

"Very temporarily. You'd have to smoke it 24/7 for any measurable benefit."

"Can do!"

"And intense smoking diminishes the flow of oxygen to the eye, further damaging the optic nerve. So you'd be worse off than when you started. Only higher."

Some students wanted to see the treated eye. "There's nothing to see," Nash said. "The procedure doesn't change the appearance of the eye at all."

Three boys examined it anyway. They approached Nash and somberly stared close into his face. Nash removed his glasses and remained motionless for the inspection, as he had for the laser, looking into the indefinite distance. The class hushed. Finally, one of them declared, "There *is* a difference. The right's opened more than the left."

Nash doubted that this was true. Kara hadn't noticed anything and he had looked in the mirror himself. But the youth was serious. One of the other students murmured confirmation. Nash conceded, "Maybe there's some swelling. The vision is still unfocused." He closed his left eye. "I can hardly see out of it."

He was unsettled by the students' observations. Perhaps he hadn't noticed the swelling after the operation because, lamentably, he had been too squeamish to study his own eye. He closed his left eye again. The classroom turned soft and grayish.

Nash had been sent to the glaucoma specialist by his regular eye doctor, who had detected moderately elevated pressure in both eyes during a routine examination two years earlier.

The eye doctor called Jaeger the "biggest glaucoma man" in the region, and his practice occupied an entire floor within one of the city's leviathan hospitals. The epithet had led Nash to expect a big man, and in fact Jaeger was athletically tall, with intense blue, unspectacled eyes and long, gray hair brushed back from his forehead. His grip was strong and his gaze direct.

Like many chronic conditions that could be mitigated by early detection, glaucoma disproportionately afflicted the urban poor, especially the diabetic and elderly among them. They dominated Jaeger's waiting room, their canes and walkers scattered like toys in a child's playroom, their cataracts flooding. Some were feeble, and many were obese or at least overweight, and some reeked of age. Many were nearly blind. Nash had just turned thirty-five and was clearly a professional. He was also an adventurous, expert skier who had always expected that his first encounter with specialized medicine would take place in the orthopedic ward. He returned Jaeger's handshake with a grip that was equally forceful.

He made sure that the doctor was aware that he taught science at what was considered the best high school in the city. Jaeger lived outside the city, in an affluent town that Nash said he knew well. He had friends there, in fact. He told Jaeger about Kara and their two young boys and inquired about Jaeger's own family and where his kids went to school. Nash considered it an urgent task, at his first and subsequent appointments, to break through the deadening hum of the doctor's daily routine and to distinguish himself from the hundreds of patients who shuffled anonymously through Jaeger's clinic, mostly old and unproductive, incurious and passive in the face of illness, and inured to misfortune.

Jaeger briefly responded to Nash's questions, though he remained intent on the examination. He wielded a variety of instruments, including a magnifying lens that slipped wetly onto the surface of Nash's eye. When Jaeger spoke, he didn't look him in the face, but rather at a point deep within his eyes that, Nash suspected, was not congruent with the window on his soul. The doctor was busy.

Nash asked, "Do you ski?"

Jaeger murmured something as he entered a figure into Nash's chart.

"They're already expecting snow this week. I try to get out as soon as possible."

Jaeger nodded, a minimal gesture, and then, because Nash was still waiting, he conceded. "I like skiing."

"Downhill?"

The doctor grunted in assent, removing another ophthalmic device from a drawer.

But neither daily medication—two drops in each eye every morning and evening—nor strenuous schmoozing controlled Nash's glaucoma, and Jaeger eventually confirmed that laser surgery would be necessary in the right eye, where tests showed the vision was deteriorating. He offered the diagnosis with little feeling. Nash would have preferred for the doctor to express more sympathy for his condition, but understood that Jaeger told patients they required surgery every day. Anyway, it was a minor ailment, easily treated with an outpatient procedure that was the specialist's bread and butter. He could do it the following week.

As a concession to Nash's interest in science, Jaeger brought him to the surgery room and showed him the laser, a profusely knobbed apparatus clad in medical beige. He invited Nash to sit in the chair and lean forward into the instrument's chin rest. Nash recalled the exotic allurements of laser technology before the devices were made ubiquitous in CD players and other appliances. He told Jaeger that in college he had been part of a student physics workshop that built one from scratch.

"Cool," Jaeger said.

It had been a helium-neon unit; as they installed the vacuum tube, the shimmering dichroic mirrors, and the electrical power panel, the students were aware of the audacity in their intention to summon from inert elemental gases the primeval energy trapped within their quantum binds. Constructed on a worktable from scavenged parts, the device would transmit a coherent beam of intense visible light for only fifteen minutes before the transformer smoked and expired, but in that quarter of an hour the young men saw themselves at the questing edge of science.

In Nash's first follow-up visit after the operation, the doctor produced a penlight and shone it deep into the treated eye, inspecting it for defects. He flicked the beam into the eye and then away and observed its dilation reflexes. He measured the treated eye's pressure. A probe tipped with a glowing green sphere approached Nash, swelled, and disappeared into greenness. It had touched down on the surface of his right eyeball. It had planted a flag and collected minerals. He never felt the probe, though he knew it was there. The surface of the eye was as nerveless as the moon's. The doctor repeated the pressure examination on his left eye.

"Fifteen," Jaeger said, with what sounded like a faint tantara of triumph. "Thirteen in the left."

"That's good," Nash said casually, trying to match Jaeger's restraint. The right eye had been as high as 20, 20 mmHg. That meant the pressure had been equivalent to what was necessary to raise a column of mercury twenty millimeters.

"It may drop further. Continue with the medication in both eyes. We want to bring down the left too. I should see you in a month."

"Sure, I'll make an appointment up front," Nash said, as Jaeger handed him his chart. "But, you know, the vision in the right eye hasn't cleared yet." Nash closed the other eye. The doctor was shadowed by a gray haze sweeping down from the left. The expression on his face become indistinct; the effect was of a man in motion. "It's very blurred. You're blurred."

"The eye's healing. That's normal."

Nash opened his left eye. "It's been more than a week."

"Some eyes take longer to heal. The mystery of individual variation," Jaeger added ironically. "It looks like it's doing nicely and the pressure's down."

"All right."

"Come back in a month and we'll look at it again."

The doctor turned to leave. His practice operated at full throttle: right now more than a dozen residents, fellows, students, and technicians were preparing patients for their moment with the glaucoma specialist or taking them away after their moment had passed. At least four exam rooms were always occupied.

"Actually," Nash said, sliding forward to rise from the deep chair. It took a moment. "There's one more thing I need to ask you about."

The doctor had already stepped from the room. He turned and leaned toward Nash, but his feet remained planted in the hall. An assistant passed quickly on her way somewhere else and looked up, briefly wondering what had delayed the doctor's rounds.

"Yes, Mr. Nash?"

"I taught a lesson on the procedure to my physics class. Great bunch of kids, very sharp. One of them observed that the right eye is now slightly larger than the left. I hadn't noticed it myself until he mentioned it."

Jaeger gazed into Nash's face through the doorway. "Yes, it's enlarged," he confirmed. "That's to be expected."

Nash laughed to show his relief. "Okay, that's great. It's just, you know, something you hadn't told me to expect."

"The eye has suffered a trauma. Swelling of the affected tissue is the usual response."

"Of course," Nash said. *Trauma* was not a word the doctor had used before. "It'll revert to normal?"

Jaeger pushed out his lower lip for a moment. "I would think so. Keep taking your drops and I'll see you in a month. Now, if you'll excuse me . . ."

Nash wouldn't report the exchange back to his sixth-period class or to his wife. Leaving the examination room, he repeatedly closed and opened his left eye, aware of the transformation of the world's light and substance. A fluorescent glare streaked from the receptionists' station into the beige-and-white waiting area. In the elevator the illuminated buttons danced on the panel like Christmas ornaments. In the dusk the parking lot's overhead lamps had come on hot and needle-edged. *I would think so . . .*

As Jaeger had predicted, Nash's vision in his right eye seemed to improve over the next few weeks. He became comfortable driving again. His concern for his eyesight joined the list of quotidian worries intrinsic to a life kept full by family and career. Yet from time to time, usually while driving, he found himself testing the right eye and wondered how much the vision had really cleared. He observed a marked difference between what he saw from the two eyes; had that difference been there before the procedure? Perhaps the right eye hadn't improved at all since the operation and he had only acclimatized himself to his vision loss. The eye was still enlarged, his students said.

Nash was gratified by their attentiveness. This was a class of earnest young people excited less by the actual content of the lesson units than by Nash's emphasis on the scientific method. The method, he told them, expanded human awareness. It defended independence of thought and the individual himself. It made a cold, chaotic universe comprehensible. The kids understood. All you had to do was observe. Observe, hypothesize, predict, experiment. These words were emblazoned on banners above the blackboard. They would be on the test.

At the next checkup, he greeted Jaeger warmly and asked after his family. Then, adopting a more professional manner, Nash said, "Perhaps there's some progress, but I don't think the eye's returned to where it was before the operation."

"You have to be patient with it."

"It's been five weeks," Nash noted, strenuously avoiding complaint.

Jaeger nodded absently, as if he didn't realize that it could have been a complaint. Nash wondered if the doctor was lonely in his ophthalmologic practice, where he was companioned entirely by underlings. They always followed him by several paces; they turned toward him to catch every word. Nash couldn't imagine that they could carry on an ordinary conversation with him about anything. Jaeger said now, "The eye is a delicate organ. It has to recover."

"I hope it does." Nash heard the fear in his own voice for the first time. This was no longer an academic exercise or a scientific adventure. He blurted, "I'm worried about the eye! Both eyes! What if I lose my vision?"

Jaeger smiled. "That's why you're here. That's what we're trying to prevent."

"Can I go blind?"

"No. There's very little chance of that."

"How little?"

"I don't know. Five percent?"

Five percent was a small chance, but hardly a remote one. Five percent was a tangible, real-world, easily imaginable possibility. You wouldn't eat a piece of meat if it had a 5 percent chance of making you sick. You wouldn't maneuver your car into a tight space if you had a 5 percent chance of denting the fender. Nash had bet on horses with worse chances, and a couple had come in. Once, years ago, when he considered the possible outcomes of several career-advancement paths, he had ranked eventually becoming a high school principal at about 5 percent. The exercise had given him hope. The principal's chair had seemed attainable, worth striving for. This new, equivalent possibility now generated despair.

"Twelve in both eyes," Jaeger said, after checking the pressure. "Not too shabby, Michael."

The doctor seemed truly pleased by the number, a familiar, two-digit integer. He penciled it into Nash's chart. "Twelve. Twelve," he murmured. He offered the patient a handshake, which, despite his surprise, Nash immediately accepted. Jaeger was pleased with Nash for persevering through years of examinations, medications, and then the uncomfortable procedure. The doctor had called him by his first name. Nash recognized, however, that the purpose of the treatment had not been to lower a number. Jaeger had neither restored Nash's eyesight nor halted its deterioration. Five percent was another number. Nash held his tongue, however, holding on to the moment of camaraderie.

Vision was a subjective experience. What you viewed through your own eyes could never be communicated. You employed approximations and commonplace concepts, such as color and shape, but these abstractions never summed the totality of what you saw, which remained rooted in your intimate, personal sensation of reality. Myriad qualities composed a moment's sight: contrast, shade, light, texture, dimensionality, color, and motion. Maybe something else too. No list could describe all the components of vision, and no words could adequately describe variations in these qualities for the purposes of diagnosis and treatment. A number was the only fact on which a practitioner could seize, even if the number was irrelevant.

Late that winter, Nash took the family on a skiing vacation. The days were pleasant, and the boys, without fear of the slopes or the other skiers, poleless and still on short skis, made great advances. On Sunday afternoon Nash took off on his own to run a few black diamond trails. The light was just starting to fade. The powder had begun to assume its late-day resilience, occasionally crunching under his skis. Coming down fast near the end of a run, he didn't notice a small ice patch, didn't make the necessary semiconscious adjustments, and he nearly spilled.

It was only a moment's lost grace. As he continued his run, hardly diverted, he tried to remember what he had seen of the ice and why he had missed it. That section of the trail, a short jog to the right at the end of a long chute, had clearly been visible down to its ruts and creases. The snow appeared in shades of white and gray. A slippery patch would have shown as something whiter, perhaps reflective.

The bottom of the mountain spread out before him as he emerged from the trail, the lodge lights flaming orange smears. The snow turned blue. He was passed by other skiers muffled in mist. Beyond the lodge lay the parking lot and a landscape of mountains and woods for miles upon miles. All were pale blue-gray, almost transparent, the entire planet a phantasm buoyant within the plasma sea surging between his cornea and his optic nerve.

Kara sympathized. He found her with their sons at the ski racks. "It's getting near dusk," she said. "I'm having trouble seeing too. Everyone does."

"I know. But I think I'm seeing worse than last year. I can't prove it, but that's my sense. I nearly fell."

"But I *did* fall! On my butt." She showed him the powder running up her side. She was not, however, as skilled a skier as he was. "A total wipeout."

A series of examinations over the next year showed the degraded vision in his right eye holding steady, more or less, while the left eye showed signs of field loss. For the test, Nash was required to sit before an open white box, one or the other eye covered, and press a joystick every time a light flashed somewhere on the illuminated screen within the box. Sometimes the flashes were faint, and sometimes he didn't see them at all, and sometimes, he realized moments later, he pressed the button after he had only imagined a flash. The exam required about fifteen minutes per eye.

After the third or fourth test that year, the technician said that he should return to the waiting room. The doctor would speak to him about his results, and Nash replied, "No, they're my results. I'll look at them myself."

The technician shrugged. He tore off the sheet of thermal paper emerging from the machine and handed it still warm and damp to Nash. While the young man slouched heavy-lidded in his chair with his legs swung apart, Nash studied the two charts, one for each eye, with each retinal field diagrammed in a quadrisected circle. The circle for the left eye was mostly clear, save for the troubling digitized square patches in the lower left quadrant, which represented regions of his retina that had not registered the light flashes, imaginary or otherwise. The right eye was much worse. Clouds of gray and black scudded across the circle, with a heavy mass gathering within the upper nasal quadrant, between the center of his vision and the northwest horizon.

Jaeger continued to express guarded satisfaction with Nash's intraocular pressure, which hovered between 11 and 14. Nash confined his protests to murmurs and vague, rueful demurrals that the doctor didn't feel obliged to answer. Nash believed he had lost something in his total vision that didn't show up in Jaeger's measurements, neither in the pressure tests nor in the visual field tests. The deficiency presented itself as a kind of attenuation of reality, as if space, or the opposite of space, whatever that could possibly be, was insinuating itself between the atoms of perception.

Because the hospital was affiliated with a graduate school, residents and students were often present at Jaeger's examinations; the doctor occasionally gave impromptu lectures on the details of Nash's condition, to which Nash gave his full attention. Once, after photographs of his retinas had been taken, he was the subject of a small conference-room seminar. He sat in on the discussion, sipping coffee he had poured from the office coffeemaker. He gravely nodded as if he were one of the personnel and as if he understood the full substance of Jaeger's remarks. He studied the pictures as they were passed around: His right eye was incandesced the color of the setting sun. An uneven network of blood vessels converged on a small disk, the optic nerve, in the center of the sphere, where much of the glaucoma-related damage was taking place. The doctor had introduced Nash in a complimentary way as a patient deeply interested in his treatment. Or was Jaeger being condescending? Nash asked what he believed were concise, collegial questions.

He looked around the table at the young people in lab coats, not much older than his students. They seemed bright, attentive, and serious in purpose.

Nash commented, "You should be aware that trabeculoplasty has an uneven success rate. It doesn't always work out. It can make things worse." He smiled generously. "As Dr. Jaeger notes, the pressure dropped in my right eye after laser surgery. That was the successful aspect of the procedure. But the eye never repaired itself after the surgical trauma." Nash closed his left eye and slowly passed his hand in front of his face from right to left. The hand vanished as it crossed the plane of his nose. "My vision has not come back to where it was before the surgery."

Nash's remarks and his prestidigitation, which only he could observe, were met with several moments of silence. The students looked to Jaeger for a response

The doctor unhurriedly looked at Nash's chart. "Yes, you've lost some of your visual field since the surgery. That's from your glaucoma, which we're still trying to control. Nothing was lost in the surgery itself. That's what the record shows."

"The record's incorrect!"

"We've found that after surgery some patients become more *conscious* of their eyesight. They only believe they're seeing less."

Nash muttered, "That's scientific."

"We've done objective tests," Jaeger said, ignoring the sarcasm. "The results are conclusive. The procedure stabilized your vision loss."

"And I believe you're missing something, some quality in human vision that's not recordable in your set of tests." Nash turned to the residents and students for support. Some heat started to show in his face, though he continued to speak lightly, with a faint, amused, deliberately fixed smile. "That's why trabeculoplasty was a failure for this individual patient."

"The procedure has a very high success rate," Jaeger declared. "The side effects are minimal."

Nash recognized that nearly all doctors, including Dr. Jaeger, offered their treatment in good faith, sincerely believing they were helping their patients. Nash wondered, though, if the practitioners allowed for the potential that the established treatments they employed could be mistaken. Did they admit their fallibility? Did they *embrace* their fallibility? Probably not. A certain amount of arrogance must be required to cut through vital human tissue, or to offer medication, or to shoot a high-intensity beam of coherent light into someone's eye. If they were afraid or lived in doubt, then they would be unable to offer treatment at all.

Nash demanded, "Did you record that the vision in my right eye failed after the surgery?"

"It didn't."

Nash threw up his hands. "If you don't record your failures, how can you possibly know the procedure's true success rate?"

The students and residents stared at Nash's hands as if they were the organs that were the object of medical intervention. Jaeger closed Nash's chart, a signal to his junior colleagues that they could assemble their things.

Unperturbed by Nash's outburst, Jaeger said, "Thank you, Michael. We don't always get the patient's perspective."

He repeated the conversation to Kara that evening. She said, "Find another doctor. Get a second opinion. You should have switched doctors years ago."

Nash looked away. The suggestion was so obviously correct, yet in all his meditations about his condition, in all his questioning and diligence, the thought of leaving Jaeger had never occurred to him. *Nash* was fallible, that was for sure. The most sensible way forward could lie right before him, but his accustomed patterns of thinking obscured it as surely as any visual defect.

"I can't switch," he said. "I don't think the problem is with Jaeger per se. The medication and the laser surgery are accepted practices in the field, and anyone will prescribe the same thing. And I *like* Jaeger. I think he's smart. He knows me, he knows my history. He has all my records. He listens to me. Anyway, the damage is done." Nash spread his hands in appeal. "I don't know what to do."

"Glad we have insurance," she said. "I'd hate to be paying for this."

Nash now established a regular cycle of visits to Jaeger's office, around the equinoxes. Every six months the doctor checked Nash's pressure and a technician administered a visual field test. Nash greeted Jaeger warmly every time. He asked about his family and his upcoming ski trips. The furniture and wall hangings in the examination rooms became as familiar and invisible as those in his classroom, while the technicians and residents were new from visit to visit. Jaeger's practice saw staff turnover like a convenience store's, save for the receptionists, who seemed to have been there since before the doctor himself.

The right eye's vision remained about the same, though over several appointments Jaeger continued to track deterioration of the visual field in Nash's left eye. Nash studied the charts. The decline wasn't consistent from test to test. They would occasionally see an apparent uptick, but he understood that this didn't signify an actual restoration of his visual field, a physiological impossibility, but was rather the result of his varying attentiveness at the time of each test. He wondered if the field loss in the left eye could be solely attributed to the decline in his alertness as he aged. Was that taken into account? And how about the time of day in which he had taken the tests, or whether they were conducted before or after lunch, and how about the number of cups of coffee he had consumed? There were many variables, and the doctor hardly considered them all.

Nash had no idea how much Jaeger's increasingly esoteric examinations of his visual field, his acuity, his depth perception, the condition of his retinas, and his corneal thickness were costing his insurance company. He suspected that the average visit totaled several hundred dollars or more than a thousand. The trabeculoplasty must have cost many thousands. The teachers' union health plan covered everything, but money still changed hands, somehow, so mysteriously that not even Jaeger could be aware exactly how much any individual patient was contributing to his bank account. The figure would appear in some column of numbers unseen by human eyes. The opacity of the charges paralleled the opacity of the medical interventions.

Nash's eyeglass prescription was changed every few years, but each time, after the initial few weeks' refreshment, he sensed that the world had subsided into its previous muddle. He was now aware of a strain when he drove, especially after dark, and he often gave the wheel to Kara, who didn't care for driving at night either. He needed perfect illumination to read a book and couldn't do it with as much fluency and pleasure as he once did. His friends of the same age voiced similar complaints about their eyesight. Frustration entered Nash's voice when he explained that his difficulties were the result of a specific condition. He was aware, of course, that friends and loved ones lived with seriously disabling illnesses, while he was only becoming more tentative on the ski slopes.

Jaeger increased Nash's medication dosage. He administered the drops to both eyes twice a day. He lay on his back on the bed, gently pulling down his lower eyelid to create a small pocket inside it. The medicated tears splashed down from on high and welled there, thoroughly soaking the eyeball. This ritual had once seemed like an interesting little facet of what it meant to be Michael Nash. Now it was a dull labor that he was sentenced to perform every day for the rest of his life. He recalled from time to time that his regular eye doctor had only *suggested* he see the glaucoma specialist. He'd never said that his elevated pressure required urgent attention.

Nash continued to teach the mechanics of laser technology. The school purchased a demonstration laser for the science department. He turned off the classroom lights. Attended by several brushed-steel boxes of electronic components, the long, glass discharge tube glowed crimson and emitted a pencil of light, a classic death ray. Every year he told the story of his surgery, in a lesson about the laser's therapeutic uses. The lesson also demonstrated that medical practice was not the same as the practice of science. The right eye's failure to recover from surgery had never been entered into the professional database; no protocol required that the fact be entered. He shut his left eye and, passing his hand in front of his face, he showed his students where the vision ended in his right eye. It marked the border between empirical evidence and conventional medical treatment.

His right eye remained slightly larger than his left, though the difference was so slight, no one ever commented on it. He was sufficiently vain not to mention it to his wife.

Winter break ended and Nash's first-period students shuffled into his classroom, crashing into each other and into the desks, dropping their textbooks, stomping their boots, and, with uncharacteristically fine motor precision, occupying the same seats that they had claimed in September. He stood at the front of the room, accepting their New Year's greetings.

As he waited for them to settle, Nash recalled the individuals in the class, its stars and clowns, the hard workers and the slackers, those who needed encouragement and those whose interest in science was not yet excited. He gazed at them and realized that although he could identify who the students were by their locations in the classroom, and also by their general appearances, their faces remained indistinct, each hardly more than a blur of eyes, nose, lips, and mouth. He checked that the lights were on and that the window blinds were up. Everything was normal.

The students quieted, but Nash continued to study them. Some of the faces came into focus, especially those attached to the bigger personalities, but most did not. He wondered how long ago they had started to lose definition. In the fall? Five years ago? He understood, however, that the phenomenon was not entirely caused by his field loss. Thousands of students had passed through his classroom in what was becoming a long, successful career. He considered himself no less dedicated than he had been in his first years, but now he was more aware of the repetitiveness built within the school calendar and in the lessons themselves, and he was aware too of the predictability of the students' needs, their struggles, and their achievements. As the students stared at him in expectation, awaiting the first words of the year's first lesson, Nash felt that he was bumping against some kind of wall. It was a wall of slightly smudged glass.

At his next appointment with Jaeger, Nash reported that his field loss seemed to be progressing.

Jaeger examined his chart. "Yes, your pressure's up in the left eye. You're not responding to medication. The next step is surgery."

"Laser surgery? Trabeculoplasty?"

"There's discomfort, but it's a relatively painless procedure."

"I know. You did my right eye six years ago!"

Jaeger flipped through several pages in the folder, which was several inches thick. He was looking for confirmation.

"Right," he said, his head down in the chart. He didn't remember. Nash was stunned. "So you know what's involved. You'll be in and out in an hour."

"I'd like to just stick with the medication."

The doctor shook his head as if the medication had suddenly become a quack remedy. "The procedure's very effective."

"Not for me it wasn't."

Jaeger continued to travel back through Nash's folder. "Your pressure in your right eye was twenty. After the surgery it dropped to twelve. There's no reason to think we can't achieve comparable results in the left."

Nash rolled both afflicted orbs. "The pressure went down, but the vision became worse!"

"That's not what your chart says."

Nash spoke in a measured voice, congratulating himself for his composure: "Actually, it's *your* chart."

The doctor's steady gaze was naked to the world, unmediated by eyeglasses or, it appeared, by contact lenses. Jaeger had never experienced surgery, or medication, or any but the most basic ophthalmic examination. Nash wondered how the perfectly sighted such as Jaeger conceived of a limit on another person's vision. They might have understood it only through simile—as gauze or a screen before one's face, for instance—and not believe in it as a real physiological phenomenon. Even as they took apart and reassembled other people's fragile, intricate optic machinery, they would find it hard to believe in a difference between the world that is and the world that's seen.

"I can only go by what the chart says, Michael. You know, we've found that after surgery some patients become more conscious of their eyesight than they were before. They may *think* their eyesight's worse."

"So I've heard! And people only *thought* the leeches were killing them. Tell me, Leonard, how do you differentiate between real and imagined vision loss?"

"Tests," Jaeger said, curt and thin-lipped. "All we can do are objective, scientific tests."

"Your tests are incomplete. And I can't afford to lose the vision in my left eye. I won't accept surgery again."

Jaeger didn't shrug, it wasn't in his nature. But he said, "That's your choice, of course. If you refuse aggressive measures to bring down your pressure, Michael, I don't see how I can help you further."

Now Nash showed anger. "Are you refusing to treat me?"

Now Jaeger did shrug. "I don't know what else I can do for you."

Nash leveled his index finger at him. "But you acknowledge that the first trabeculoplasty failed."

"It lowered your pressure."

"And damaged my eyesight. And now you're cutting me loose. Once I walk out that door"—Nash moved his finger in the direction of the elevators—"the evidence of my vision loss will vanish. The *memory* of it will vanish. When other patients report the same problems, you'll discount their complaints. You'll keep performing the same surgery in the same way."

Jaeger closed the folder and presented it to his patient, to bring to the front desk. "I suppose I will. We're very confident that the procedure stabilizes patients' intraocular pressure."

Nash snatched the chart from the doctor and exited the treatment room. He rushed down the long corridor, his steps echoing like ricochets off the tile, past the open doors of other treatment rooms. There seemed to be hundreds of them. He had occupied every one, at one visit or another, in one year or another. Men and women waited for Jaeger in them now, gazing hopefully through the doorways. When Nash finally reached the receptionist's desk, he threw down the folder as if it were a losing hand.

The woman didn't observe his vehemence. "Would you like to make another appointment, Mr. Nash?"

"In six months," he said, his voice clotted. "For my regular checkup."

He would see Dr. Jaeger again in the fall, after a summer in which he would miss a step coming out onto the patio, spraining an ankle, and not recognize Kara walking toward him in the street, and have trouble making out the sign for the next highway exit, and fail to observe the Perseid meteors, and be hit in the face by a softball tossed by his older son. "Dad, are you okay? That catch was *easy*!" He would continue to visit Dr. Jaeger, if only to haunt him with the failure of the doctor's treatment, well into the ever-dimming forever.

THE UN-

There were hundreds of ways to go crazy wanting to be a writer, and as a young man Joshua Glory learned them all. He learned that you could go crazy worrying about your origins: Josh didn't know of a single great writer who had emerged from suburban mire as pedestrian as his. You could go crazy imitating the early lives of great writers—for example, seeking adventure, romance, danger, and alienation. You could go crazy moving to the far side of a slum adjacent to the bohemian neighborhood of a prohibitively expensive city and trying to write while taking on dull, derisively paid jobs on the fringes of the fringes of the fringes of writing (passing out handbills for a semiprofessional theater, telephone polling, proofreading event listings for a free weekly newspaper). You could go crazy searching for the perfect desk. You could go crazy arranging the desk's position to provide you with the softest, brightest light and the most inspiring view either of the pinched, cracked street or of the single shelf of your paperback library. You could go crazy scrutinizing how-to books for the single secret key to literary success purposely concealed, kabbalah-like, within them. You could go crazy trying to write in the style of an author you admired. You could go crazy trying *not* to write in the style of an author you admired. You could go crazy trying to explain to other people what you were working on. You could go crazy worrying that someone else was writing something similar to what you were writing and would publish it the very day you finished your final draft. You could go crazy thinking that what you were writing would be read by total strangers or, even worse, by your parents. You could go crazy thinking that it would not be read at all.

You could go nuts rereading your work, over and over, until the words were dissolved of meaning. You could unbalance yourself rewriting, trying to find the absolutely correct and precise phrase that would express what was, unfortunately, only a fuzzy idea. You could go bonkers trying to get the attention of some agent, any agent, or of some editor, any editor, or of some published writer, any published writer, even a lousy one, who could help get you published. Looking for nuance in letters of rejection would cross your eyes, loosen your screws, and displace your marbles, especially if the letters were form letters. An entire ward at the Home for the Literary Insane was occupied by people who insisted on favorably likening their evening-and-weekend scribbling to the work of the world's most accomplished writers. Another ward was for people who compared their work to that of inferior writers who were nevertheless published; something snapped when they tried to account for the appearance of these mediocrities in print: it required a bloodlessly cynical theory of publishing or, even more, a nihilist's genuflection before the mechanisms of an amoral universe. You could go crazy waiting for inspiration. You could go crazy searching for a true indication of your talent.

You could go crazy waiting for the mail. Josh stared at the mail slot across the room this morning, waiting for it to disgorge its acknowledgment that he was, indeed, a writer. It could come anytime in the late morning or the early afternoon, if not later, or if not earlier. Every day there was hope, and that hope stretched the day into a desert of time without horizon.

Now, with a few scraps of his hardly begun novel scattered on his desk next to his sea-foam-blue portable typewriter, Josh's impatience was even greater than usual. The novel whose sentences had been eminently legible to his mind just the day before had vanished like a fair-weather cloud. He had filled up page after page with notes, but none were part of the novel as he had conceived it. Several of the plot developments he had counted on were illogical or self-contradictory. The whole idea of the book now seemed preposterous.

If only he were already a published author, how much easier writing would be. If only he had a first novel on the shelf, how pleasurable it would be to write the second, the third, and the twenty-seventh. Then he'd have the confidence to sit down and work without the distracting suspicion that what he wrote was completely worthless or perhaps malign. He would be assured that his words would inevitably appear in print, between covers. Now the vast bulk of his oeuvre was only in photocopied samizdat, passed on to relatives and friends. In response, they offered cautious praise while Josh pressed them to tell him "what you really think." And even when they told him, and praised him, he wondered if they were lying and, later, behind his back, laughing or sadly shaking their heads.

So he waited for the mail to confirm that he was on the right track: the mail had been entrusted with his short stories, his first chapters, his book outlines, his critical and political essays, his "casuals" and "occasionals," his nature meditations, his article proposals, his travel accounts, his op-eds, and, most recklessly, his verse. He hoped that today it would repay his tender devotion with a letter of acceptance.

He stared at the mail slot, then out the window, then momentarily at the typewriter, then back at the mail slot, and through the window again. Something eclipsed the far end of the trash-can-lined alley across the street, which ran in shadow to the next block. He replayed the blur several times through his mind, trying to identify within it the glitter of a key chain and the smear of color that represented the national postal service.

The mailman's route on the next block, Josh had discovered the week he moved in, carried him past the opening to the alley precisely sixteen minutes before he turned onto Josh's street and reached his door. The transit, however, occurred in less than a second and was easy for Josh to miss if he was not staring through the window down the alley at the time, and even easier for him to worry that he had missed it. His vigilance, he morosely admitted, was excessive. It was not unusual for him to suffer at least one or two false alarms every day. After every false sighting he would involuntarily count off the sixteen minutes, aware that he couldn't credit it as productive work time. Once the period elapsed, he would suffer another two minutes of disappointment, tension, and deflation.

But if he missed the mailman's actual approach and never thought about it, then the carrier's arrival would be a happy surprise, the letters and magazines exploding through his door slot. Josh maintained a superstitious belief that his best mail days—that is, days in which the rejection slips were faintly encouraging, individually written letters—were ones in which he hadn't anticipated the mail's arrival at all, as if the creative spark that had lit the idea for a short story and the agonizing care he had taken to execute it were less important than not remembering the daily postal delivery. He consulted his digital watch, which lay on the desk between his notes and his typewriter. Three minutes had passed since he had seen the mailman, or thought he had seen him.

Josh had once owned a standard windup clock, but the ticking bothered him. Or rather, it wasn't the ticking that bothered him, but the pauses between the ticks: he found himself waiting for the next tick (just as he was now waiting for the mailman). He knew this was ridiculous, that a real writer immersed in his work wouldn't notice a church bell going off in his study.

He stared now at the watch for a moment longer and then out the window, and then back at the typewriter. He wrote two sentences, neither of which, strangely enough, had to do with mailmen or church bells, but with his novel. They were wonderful sentences, and he further saw the shape of the two sentences after them—their syntax and meter, if not the actual words—plus that of the plot several pages ahead. Exhilarated, he began typing the third sentence, but its phrasing momentarily stymied him. Josh glanced at the watch and saw that this burst of creativity had consumed nine minutes, for a total of twelve since he had first seen the mailman (if that was who it was) at the end of the alley.

The hell with the mail. Josh would gladly have allowed whatever items the mailman was to deliver within the next four minutes to molder inside the door, nearly at his desk, unexamined the rest of the week, if he could occupy that time as lost in composition as he had just been. *I'm concentrating*, he told himself. *I'm writing!*

Josh arrived at this congratulatory thought halfway through the third sentence, by which time it was no longer true. He stared at the sentence, completed it, and regretted that its predicate had neither the fluency nor the heft that he had originally envisioned. Another few minutes passed. He made a space to begin another sentence. He reread the paragraph so far. It was all right. But what was next?

And where was the mailman? The sixteen minutes had come and gone. The carrier should have arrived by now, even if he had been delayed between the other block and this one by a package or registered letter. Josh considered stepping outside to look for him, but that would have been a sure jinx, if the mailman was still on his way, against an abundant postal harvest. And it would do nothing to increase his literary output. But to continue to wait was also a formidable distraction; let's face it, he wasn't doing any writing now and could hardly locate in the frontal space of his consciousness exactly what he was working on.

Josh pushed his chair back, walked across the room, and opened the door. It was the first time he had been outside today. The flood of fresh air was a taunt. He looked up and then down the unswept little street, which was lined with wounded automobiles parked on fractured sidewalks stained by spilled oil. At the end of the block was the mailman, who had passed by Josh's door without stopping.

Josh hadn't received anything, not even an advertising circular. This was unprecedented. His subscriptions to several magazines and literary journals hadn't won him special consideration as a potential contributor, but they guaranteed a nearly constant inflow of periodicals and placed him on mailing lists that generated further subscription offers. Plus he received the normal human allotment of utility bills. But today, for the first time since he'd moved here, the cycles of magazine delivery, subscription campaigning, utility billing, submission rejection, and personal correspondence had met in a perfectly congruent trough.

If something had come, Josh would probably have been disappointed with it, but at least he would have been satisfied that the day's mail had given him a fair shake. No mail at all simply prolonged by another twenty-four hours the waiting for mail that should have come today.

Josh watched the back of the mailman for a few minutes as he delivered to his neighbors *their* acceptances, *their* galleys, and *their* royalty checks.

You could go so crazy wanting to be a writer that the struggle to get published became the principal theme of your life and work. You could lose interest in family dynamics, the legacy of history, the interplay of chance and destiny, the bitter mysteries of romantic love, and the costs of personal ambition, all dependably productive literary themes. You could find yourself disinclined to read literature that grappled with ordinary human affairs or to talk with friends about sporting events, politics, and their personal dramas. You could become concerned instead only with what it meant to be an unpublished writer. You could find yourself writing about this obsession, trying to distill the compromises and humiliations and false victories you had endured into a single narrative testimony. Mostly you could want to express your sense that in Creation there was but a single Wall, the Wall that separated the published from the un-, and that somehow getting over it, around it, or through it was the only worthwhile human endeavor. You could make up a character intent on overcoming this barrier, a character very much like yourself, though perhaps one a touch less delusional.

With the possibility of receiving an acceptance today extinguished, Josh fell into a black mood, sure that he would never see another line in print again.

He had written eight short stories that he considered worthy of publication. One of them had appeared two years earlier in a small literary quarterly that had since folded, published by a university that then lost its accreditation, located in a state that shortly afterward seceded from the Union.

The other stories were currently lying in seven cartons in the offices of seven journals whose names Josh had expunged from his short memory out of an elaboration of his belief that success would come only as a surprise. Having decided that they were publishable, Josh wouldn't allow the stories to remain at home. When one came back rejected, he sent it out again that day, restoring within hours the manuscript's acceptance to the realm of the possible.

There was a limit to how often he could bear to do this. After a short story had been returned ten or twelve times—in envelopes treacherously addressed by his own hand, the stamps affixed with his own self-defeating saliva—it acquired a patina of rejection through which he could hardly read the words. Every doubt he had ever entertained about the story was magnified; every difficult decision he had ever made about character formulation, plot development, or word choice was shown to be a mistake.

Josh never submitted a story to more than one publication at a time. For one thing, he didn't want to offend the publishing authorities, who not only frowned upon this practice but, according to the literary self-help books, condemned writers to anonymity for lesser infractions—these included sending a title page with the manuscript, sending a photocopy or carbon, single- or triple-spacing, and telephoning a publication after two or three months to inquire what had become of the manuscript.

Furthermore (and this was truly ridiculous), for all his profound doubts about the story, his disgust at the artificiality of his dialogue and the plot, his dismay at the insubstantiality of his characters, and, above all, his embarrassment at his audacity in thinking that he was a writer, at the moment Josh dropped the manuscript into the mailbox (and softly whispered, "Good luck"), he truly believed that the journal to which he was submitting the story would publish it. He feared that if he sent the story to, say, four literary quarterlies at the same time, all four would accept it (why shouldn't they? It was a great story), and he'd be in the uncomfortable position of having to write back to three of them to withdraw the manuscript, and who knew what editorial wrath *that* would incur? He sensed too, deep in his bones, that this confidence in the story, as ephemeral as it might have been, was an element necessary to the entire foolish enterprise.

Drawing from a different pool of emotions, Josh also sympathized with the editors of these publications. He knew that the typical editor was some underpaid, literature-loving academic sentenced to facing twenty or thirty barely readable manuscripts on the floor under *his* mail slot every day of his working life, manuscripts from desperate people who not only didn't read the obscure quarterly (circulation 300) for which he was sacrificing his eyesight, but hadn't even correctly spelled the title of the publication on their envelopes, which as likely as not arrived without return postage. Occasionally one of the editor's own rejected poems or short stories, sent back from an obscure quarterly that *he* didn't read, would be mixed in with the day's mail.

By sending out only a single carefully typed copy of each story at a time, in a meticulously addressed envelope, always accompanied by a self-addressed, stamped envelope, by buying and sometimes reading the most trivial of these quarterlies, Josh intended to improve the position of editors everywhere and, indirectly, the status of writers and, even more indirectly and speculatively, his own.

Josh learned that you could go crazy attending readings. You went with the hope that somehow, in the presence of an author, deeply immersed in the sound of his thoughtfully written prose, you might connect with literature in some intimate, inspiring way that you didn't when you were reading only to yourself or writing. Perhaps you also hoped to meet a girl.

He went to a reading that evening, at a coffee shop with smoke-stained walls and stale pastries, in a neighborhood that was trying to insinuate itself into the bohemian quarter. He didn't know anyone there, but the customers looked familiar, a representative segment of the city's continually replenished, intermittently optimistic population of would-be writers. They were mostly as young as Josh and, it seemed, indefinably more stylishly dressed.

The author's just-published clothbound books were for sale tonight, stacked alongside the podium. The author wasn't entirely famous, but his name was somewhat known, though perhaps it was confusable with the name of another writer slightly better known. His novel had been favorably reviewed in the weekly paper and a few other fringy publications, infusing it with the glow of artistic nonconformism.

Tall, athletic, his hair flecked with silver, his face etched by the years, the author shyly thanked the audience for coming. He told a self-deprecating anecdote about how he had begun writing the novel. The audience laughed. His manner was easy as he began reading. He looked up often, as if he weren't reading at all, but as if he were only now composing the text. His eyes sparkled, reflecting his evident pleasure in the language. From time to time he puckishly rubbed his face. The crowd was hooked from the very first line. Around the coffee shop, men and women beamed. The women found him irresistibly attractive.

Josh was riveted, imagining that it was he himself who towered behind the podium. Although he had always been too severely afflicted with stage fright to perform even in high school theater productions, Josh believed that once he was published, he would be capable of matching the author's dramatic effects and winningly comfortable demeanor. Josh's eyes would brighten in the presence of an audience. He too would turn his mouth into an engaging, demure, sympathy-drawing half smile. He would show—sincerely, quite sincerely—just how surprised and grateful he was to have readers. He would be gallant with the ladies.

Applause and questions followed the reading. The writer was asked about his favorite authors, his sources of inspiration, his work habits, and mostly how he managed to have his novel published. That last question—how he was published—was asked several times, relentlessly, through increasingly creative locutions, indicating that the audience of would-be writers in fact harbored several repositories of literary ingenuity and wit. The author dodged the question. The audience persisted. A middle-aged woman, wrapped in a bulky raincoat, rose to declaim at length, incomprehensibly, or at least whatever comprehension could be gleaned from her speech suggested profound disappointment. She had not been published. She didn't think she would ever be published. The author tried to quiet her with a hopeful, gracious, and witty remark, but the woman had more to say, descending by steps into incoherence. Her eyes were wet. The audience tittered nervously, worried that her pleading would be associated with theirs. The author replied more vaguely, eluding her tirade. He made another joke at his own expense. He again thanked the audience for coming and there was more applause, even greater than before, as if to silence and rebuke the woman, who remained standing.

Josh buttoned his jacket and realized that, although he had been closely attentive to the author's appearance, voice, and mannerisms, as well as to his almost aphoristic responses to the questions, he couldn't recall a single detail from the man's work. He could hardly articulate his novel's theme. The novel shimmered somewhere, transparent and immaterial, behind the much more solid idea of the writer's presence—and not even his presence, but rather his condition as a published author. And it was not even his *condition* as a published author that was so compelling, but rather the promise that the condition was somehow impartable, that, through careful observation of a published author and sheer proximity to him, you might someday become a published author yourself.

Josh left the coffee shop, filing out onto the street with the rest of the crowd, and felt unsettled. After many years and much personal sacrifice, the author had finally succeeded in writing and publishing a novel. He may have fancied the novel would change the world; he may have loved the novel like a woman or a child. But Josh hardly cared about the book. He cared mostly, nearly only, about someday publishing his own novel—which the audiences attending *his* readings would hardly care about either. The author had sold one copy of his novel this evening.

You could go crazy trying to be competitive with other aspiring writers. You met them in low-life bars, at literary parties, at poetry slams, in bookstores, in magazine shops, at the library, at writing schools and writing conferences, and, inevitably, at the local grocery, where they were buying unfiltered cigarettes that you yourself weren't quite tough enough to smoke. You also met them at work.

Alberto Dreyfus-Borodin smoked unfiltered cigarettes. He wore silver wire-rimmed eyeglasses. His jaw was tipped by a glossy black goatee. His motorcycle jacket had been seasoned by the open road. A few years older than Josh, he bore a vaguely literary reputation and a dark, uncompromising gaze. He worked alongside Josh as a proofreader for the free weekly, but he had been promoted from the event listings to proofing actual articles.

Josh presumed that he had missed the moment that had given Alberto a certain cachet at the city's literary haunts. Josh would see him in a smoky corner in a bar, among several other artistic-looking people, handsome men and women. Alberto would acknowledge Josh with a brief head nod or eye flick. In the composing room where they worked, Alberto would make dismissive comments about the books being reviewed in the pages he was proofing. He had let it be known around the weekly that he was bringing to completion a massive novel of high ambition. Its substance and style unknown, the novel hung like Alberto's cigarette smoke in the imaginative space above their heads.

They were friends. Josh had given Alberto a photocopy of his most recent story on the day it was completed, the moment when its brilliance seemed most assured. He passed the sheets to him with mock ceremony, to defray the earnestness that attended his optimism. "Your life will never be the same again," he began. Two weeks later, Alberto returned the story with precisely parsed praise—"not what I necessarily would have expected," "at least it's not overly plot driven"—that Josh was still evaluating.

Tonight, after a day at his typewriter in which some fair thought seemed to gel and hover before him just beyond his grasp and was perhaps graspable if he had had but one more hour there, glossy sheets of type were coming in fast, dumped on the long, scarred wooden table that was the proofreading station. Josh lumbered down a leg of classifieds. After five minutes the agate swam before his eyes like paramecia. Proofreading was, by any standard of mid-twenties grunt work, a job of the utmost tediousness. When Josh took the position, somewhat desperately, he had hoped to spend his time at the weekly in contemplation of literary themes and important philosophical issues, while using only a few loose nerve cells to check for typos. Instead he found himself predominantly alert to circumstances in the composing room, especially the ever-shifting relations between him and his colleagues. He missed a lot of typos.

The third proofreader groaned. Both young men turned, each with a vital, hopeful, specific interest in the groan, and more generally in their co-worker's moods, their variations, their modulations, and their microgradations, which ranged from the intensely visible to the infra and ultra parts of the emotional spectrum. The colleague was a woman. Her name was Laila Makarian, and her dewy presence in the composing room three nights a week radiated waves of distraction through the pool of proofreaders, layout artists, and pressmen. She was about a year or two younger than Josh and often seemed much younger: raw-skinned, naive, a bit dazed about her insertion into adult life (just as Josh was).

Josh had offered her his story a few weeks after he had given it to Alberto. She had been so pleased that her thanks landed on him like a kiss, as sweet and soft as he had imagined a real one would be. She shook the bundle, savoring its tangibility: the fourteen numbered sheets, paper-clipped, double-spaced, his surname on the upper right-hand corner of each one except the first. With the story not yet remotely close to being published, Josh knew that any elevation in her regard was undeserved, but he appreciated it anyway. He relished how her hands gripped his manuscript. The very next day when she arrived in the composing room, before she even took off her jacket, she declared that she *loved* the story—and what a *surprise* it was! Echoing Alberto, but with much different effect, she said she would never have guessed that Josh could have written it. "It feels like it came out of nowhere," she said. Then she studied him for a few moments as she never had before, readjusting her notion of who he was. Her luminous brown eyes had always suggested something—avidity, alacrity—beyond her manifestations of guilelessness.

The praise embarrassed him. Alberto looked up from his galley, all-seeing and critical. Yet Laila's expression of astonishment stirred Josh and heightened his ardor. It meant that he had made enough of an impression for her to have an opinion about him. And that his work revealed a depth to his personality that he himself didn't know of—but that she cared for and was capable of excavating! Her comments touched him with a warmth that would permeate his being for weeks to come. He later reread the story through her eyes, imagining her responses to its literary effects, smiling where he thought she might have smiled.

Laila also wanted to be a writer, but she had struggled to articulate the kind of writing she intended to do. Fiction? Journalism? Film? Poetry? Drama? Criticism? Personal history? She wasn't sure: the question harried her. She arrived in the composing room with famous exemplars of her latest chosen genre. She read them thoroughly, critically, and delightedly; afterward she would announce another literary interest. Then she wondered whether she was meant to pioneer an entirely new, untrammeled literary territory whose horizons were yet unknown. She made notes in a little pasteboard, clothbound notebook. All she knew, she admitted, was that she wanted to call herself a writer.

This concession was rankling. Josh too was casting about for the kind of writing that most precisely suited his talents, but he preferred to believe that his literary motivations were inherently drawn from his personal character and unique vision of the world—and not merely by the desire to assume the writer's status. Laila served to remind him that he secretly doubted his purpose, while Alberto knew exactly what kind of writer he was, without having published a word.

Now, after hours of fidgeting and wincing, of pouts, micro-pouts, and nano-pouts that had touched every masculine nerve in her vicinity, Laila audibly groaned. The men turned. Alberto promptly stepped in. He asked, with suave irony, "Thine soul grows sad with troubles? Sing, and disperse them, if thou canst."

"I wish," she muttered. "Mine troubles are this job. This life."

Josh's spirits soared. He thought, *Something's wrong with your life? Change it! Go out with me!* But he didn't say that. He knew this wasn't the right time to ask her out, especially not with Alberto there; he wondered if the right time would come in this century.

He needed to say something to make up for Alberto's having spoken first. He desperately searched for a supportive response, one that would indicate his awareness of her interior life. *Thine soul grows sad*—what was that? Shakespeare or just Shakespeare-sounding? Damn! "Are you doing any writing?" he ventured tentatively, without recourse to irony, with in fact an unattractive betrayal of earnestness, but it was the best he could do. He knew writing was the key to her sense of well-being, because that was the key to his. "How's it going?"

In disgust she pushed away the galley she was proofing. "Badly. I don't know what I'm doing anymore. I start stories, but I don't finish them. I don't even finish paragraphs. I stare at the page. I'm not moved to write anything, really."

Alberto kept a thoughtful silence. This opened a door to sympathy. Josh rushed in. "That's deeply frustrating, I'm sure."

Laila declared, "I think I have writer's block."

Josh bit his lip, evaluating the statement. She was perched on her stool, turned toward him expectantly, a pencil still in her hands. Her eyes were fixed on his.

He began, "I'm not sure you can have writer's block. I mean, you know, if you haven't already been . . ."

His voice trailed off. Josh had realized how badly this had come out—how nakedly—even before her expression registered that she heard it. When his words did reach her, her face and entire posture stiffened. Laila thought that Josh meant to say that she couldn't suffer from writer's block because she hadn't yet established that she was a real writer. This was, in fact, precisely what he meant to say. Laila had no way of knowing whether she had the talent or imagination or facility with language that some mental ailment, some "block," could prevent from being exercised. Very possibly she had nothing to write. *Who did?* Her nostrils flared. Alberto stared contemptuously. Josh knew that they believed he had made the comment with the presumed authority of someone who had published a short story—although he was as aware as they were that it was only a single short story in a publication that no one read or had even heard of.

He tried to apologize. "You can't know . . . I mean, it's early. That's what I'm trying to say."

"Yeah, okay," Laila said, her face down in the galleys.

Alberto cleared his throat, commanding attention so decisively that even one of the pressmen looked up.

"There has never been a great writer who wasn't blocked," he declared, his voice a shade deeper than usual. "Blockage is the sign of a true artist unforgiving of convention and cliché. It's the sign of someone struggling to bring something new into existence. Fluency, glibness, logorrhea: that's common enough. The rare literary genius grapples honestly with the language—fiercely and courageously—and wins from it a line of type the world demands to read."

Laila's response was a tiny aspiration, wordless, nearly inaudible, more of a grunt, but deeply grateful.

Josh stared at his own galley, his ears burning. His remorse was nearly bottomless. He knew exactly how sensitive Laila was. He was sensitive too, and he would have been equally wounded by his comment. And he was superstitious. By calling Laila's talent into question, even inadvertently, he had invited the loss of any jot of ability that he might have possessed or had the potential to acquire. By being unsympathetic—unwillingly, out of awkwardness, *against every intention!*—he had called down on himself every disappointment that came with wanting to be a writer. And that was before Alberto made his helpful remarks. Josh tried to focus on the page before him. The next issue of the weekly would feature listings of events that would never occur, involving artists and performers who never existed, at least not under the unpronounceable names printed there, at venues with topographically impossible addresses, at times of day that could not be expressed by any conceivable clockface.

"I get blocked too," he muttered.

Josh learned that you could go crazy trying to get story ideas from your dreams. You could go crazy trying to get inspiration from overheard conversations on the bus. You could go crazy recording your impressions in a notebook and then trying to read them afterward. You could go crazy trying to write something great in a single caffeine-fueled night. You could go crazy trying to find the perfectly timed combination of sleep, food, alcohol, fresh air, and physical exercise that would produce the genius hour of writing.

You could go crazy as you ascended the ladder of literary disappointment. You could be disappointed that you hadn't written anything. You could be disappointed that what you had written hadn't been published. You could be disappointed that you had been published but hadn't received critical acclaim. You could be disappointed that you had received critical acclaim but hadn't won any prizes. You could be disappointed that you had won prizes, but every October were passed over for the Nobel. You could be disappointed that you had won the Nobel, but were one of those Nobelists no one ever read.

You could go crazy in bookstores. You staggered past the tables piled high with the collected wisdom of the ages, the shelves that soared to the ceiling in faith that the bursting complexity of the world could be contained by narrative text. *Could* it be contained? Or was language a limiting phenomenon, a human construction that denied existence's ineffable truths? Were these books, these objects, these primitive cardboard and paper artifacts, more than overvalued fetish objects? Was having your name on the cover of one really worth a life's devotion—the soul-destroying humiliations, the life-ruining sacrifices, the *strain*? And if the world was containable by language, then how did we know that it hadn't already been contained, by billions and billions of monkeys and their evolutionary successors banging away at their typewriters? Was there anything that you could write that was new? Weren't you only adding to the pile?

Josh wandered through the store like a derelict, stopping briefly at the remainders, then the bestseller, magazine, and cat-book sections, then drifted toward fiction, a minute fraction of the shop's geography. When he came to it, he didn't pull any novels or story collections from the shelves but merely looked at the titles, wondering at them for being there. He stopped at the wall of the *EFGH*'s. He lightly caressed their spines, moving almost unconsciously, as if he had done this many times before, which he had, to where the *G*'s were, searching for the place where a slim, stylishly written volume by a writer named Joshua Glory might squeeze in. He knew exactly on which shelf his book should be, and its absence startled him now like a missing tooth, though there was no gap at all. Gide and Goethe were flush up against each other, on guard against arrivistes.

He lightly tapped on the Gide. He touched the Goethe. He couldn't even force his finger between them.

As if the bookshop's walls and shelves had dissolved, he felt crushed by the weight of the world's literature. The books themselves unknit, spilling their words. The words churned and boiled around him. He glared at Gide and Goethe. He glared beyond them into the bookstore, at the plenitude of authors who had fought or wheedled their way into the place, many of them charlatans and hacks. Many of them plagiarists. Many of them talentless ingenues. Many of them burnouts.

Many of them lazy slobs. By what right should their books be here and by what malfeasance should his be not?

The bookstore's information desk was perhaps not equipped to provide an answer, but Josh turned there anyway. A young man in a shapeless, blue smock was behind the counter, staring into space.

"A book," Josh croaked. "I'm looking for a book."

"Unh." The clerk didn't look at him, his gaze not quite ready to relinquish its vacancy.

"The author's name is Joshua Glory."

Still not looking at him, the clerk said, "If it's not there, we don't have it."

"I know," Josh said, bowing before the syllogism. "But can you look it up anyway?"

The clerk sighed as he reached to switch on the microform reader. He asked dully, "Author's name?"

"Joshua Glory," Josh repeated. "*G* as in Gogol, *L* as in Lorca, *O* as in Orwell . . ."

Quickly, in less time than it could have possibly taken him to do the search, he said, "It's not here."

"It should be," Josh insisted.

The clerk changed microforms and gazed into the screen. "I don't see it in 'Forthcoming' either," he said grimly. "Nothing by that author."

"Are you sure? Nothing forthcoming at all?"

"Uh-uh."

Josh left the store raging, a wrathful specter that hurtled hard down the pavement and scattered oncoming pedestrians. He swore audibly. He vowed never to return, not if the store offered ruinous discounts on new hardcover books, not if it put on sale the single copy of the one book that would save his life, not if its fiction aisles were jammed with attractive, available women, not if his novel was someday heaped on the promotion tables in Everestian piles. He wanted to go home and cry, and also pound the walls and kick his desk.

He clenched his fists, he ground his teeth, yet even as he fumed, he felt upon his consciousness the gravitational tug of something else, something that was not his anger. It glowed in the vanishing distance, far from the congested city center. He tried not to look at it, but he did, and it drew him away from his anger. It was an idea. The idea was his novel, the novel in its most perfect, most ethereal, most platonic state. He slowed his pace, almost to a stop, so that he could better view the apparition. The passersby hurried around him. The encounter in the bookshop now seemed to have occurred decades ago, in another city.

The novel was almost readable, its best sentences assuming briefly definite shape. In each was a pang of pleasure, like biting into the center of a caramel, but the satisfaction was more than self-gratifying. In these ephemeral constructions something was apprehended, and the world, in a microscopically incremental way, was made more sensible and more beautiful. Then, as he took a step or two forward and several thousand words went by in a blur, the protagonists moved under their own power, for a moment. And then again when he looked at the novel as a whole, as seen from the anarchic, heedless, trivializing street, it stood for something important, at least in regard to a small fraction of existence.

Josh reached home and opened the door to his studio. The air was musty and sour from last night's cooking. The room was just as he had left it: the bed rumpled, the book he was reading askew on the end table, a letter from home folded on its back on the dinette counter with its legs up like a dead insect, and an actual dead insect. In the shadows where the walls met the ceiling, behind the few pieces of furniture scattered around the room, among the unread books and the dirty dishes in the sink, his loneliness waited for him.

The portable typewriter remained in the center of the desk, a sheet of coarse yellow paper curling up from the platen. Some notes lay alongside the machine, and on top of the papers rested a plastic pen. Josh stood over the typewriter for a while, gazing at the yellow sheet on which was typed unevenly, with cross-outs and fragmented phrases, misspelled words and errant punctuation, the three sentences that represented the first few lines of his novel. He sat down at the desk and began to tap the keys, tentatively. There were hundreds of ways to go crazy wanting to be a writer, but the only way to stay sane was to keep writing. After about sixty seconds he stopped, drummed his fingers on the desk's veneer for a few minutes, and started again. Then he stood abruptly, walked over to the window, looked out on the darkening alleyway, where a trash can had been knocked over, spilling other writers' manuscripts. Josh went back to the machine. He typed some more. After a while he had filled a page.

PROFESSOR ARECIBO

When Professor Arecibo boards the train this morning, he claims the seat opposite a copper-haired woman in a gray blazer and removes a cardboard coffee cup from a paper bag. As the train leaves the station, his regard flits across the car to the freshly shaven and cosmetically prepared faces of the other commuters, some of whom have become familiar to him over the years without the exchange of a single word or gesture. By now he thinks he knows them. He doesn't think he's seen the woman before.

He draws coffee from the cup's plastic cap and looks forward to the day. He's anticipating the report of a junior colleague who's attending a meeting in one of the government's science ministries. Arecibo is a member of the university physics faculty, a professor of radio astronomy accustomed to contemplating the electromagnetic radiation that, in a plenitude of wavelengths, pours from the heavens and inundates his everyday environment (the junior colleague, the train car, the coffee cup).

A mobile phone chirps from within the woman passenger's shoulder bag, which is resting on her lap. She withdraws the phone from the bag. He notes that her long, gracile fingers conclude in lustrous nails painted the color of rubies. She doesn't look at the number on the screen. "Hi," she says, tilting the side of her head against the device. "Good morning. How are you?" She listens for a few moments, her head cocked in the direction of the professor but her eyes unfocused, and replies, "I'm at the airport now." She adds that she will land at noon in the city to which she and Arecibo are traveling by rail. She says warmly, "I love you too," and ends the call with a decisive, almost triumphant, poke.

The professor looks away as she returns the phone to her bag. She turns from him too, gazing through the window at a distant landscape as the obscure artifacts of railroad infrastructure flicker by. He wonders if there's some misunderstanding that makes him assume that she has lied, but it's indisputable that they're not at an airport and that they're already in the grimy, haphazard outskirts of the city.

After a while Arecibo feels that by not looking at her he's making a too obviously deliberate sign of censure. He turns and gives her a casual review, almost as he would any passenger with whom he's sitting: a woman no longer young, yet younger than he is, full lipped, sharp nosed, with eyes somewhat widely set. Her metallic-red hair, possibly dyed (he's no expert on these matters), is cut short. Beneath the blazer there's a loose, open white blouse and an above-the-knee leather skirt. A canvas bag rests on the seat next to her bare legs. She's wearing heels and one of them has half slipped off, divulging the curving sweep of a smooth, taut instep. She's evidently lost in thought, but perhaps she's pretending she doesn't know that her fellow passenger has heard her blatantly lie to someone she said she loved. The professor decides she's a handsome woman, fully aware that his judgment has been corrupted by the intrigue that she has wrapped around herself like a veil.

The most plausible reason for her fabrication is that the person to whom she has just affirmed her devotion is a man who believes she's in another city, perhaps on a business trip. She hasn't traveled to that city but has remained overnight in the vicinity of this city to be with her lover. They've enjoyed illicit relations. The true history of those relations is written within and upon her body, in certain pores and crevices, in bruises and nicks, a fingernail chip, in her sweat and saliva. A microscopic bead of something foreign may still quiver on the interior of a thigh or the underside of a breast. He detects a slight puffiness in her lips, possibly the damage done by a passionate, hurried farewell at the clandestine suburban station. Arecibo senses that by exposing him to her falseness, she has given him license to imagine her intimate parts. He does this at leisure.

They eventually arrive at the central railway terminal, where Arecibo follows the woman onto the platform, attentive to her rocking, high-heeled stride, the sway of her hips and her naked calves. He allows himself to fall behind, mixing with the other disembarked passengers, but he doesn't lose sight of her. She turns her head, and a shimmer flashes off smooth, now-silky-seeming hair. She shifts the overnight bag from one hand to the other, a simple motion that illuminates a galaxy of sinew and muscle. The dent of a shoulder blade becomes momentarily evident through her jacket; also, he views a bare forearm. He slows to a complete stop, eddying the pedestrian traffic, and he's keenly aware of his own stillness within the boiling waters of the morning commute. He makes one final observation of the woman, at the entrance to the main hall, before she completely recedes into the shadows of her personal life.

The department secretary is already at her desk when he arrives, and she reminds him of the negotiations his junior colleague will pursue this morning with representatives of the international radio observatory. She hands him a stack of folders. In his office, he makes himself comfortable, checks his calendar and e-mail, and looks over the day's work, most of which depends on the outcome of the meeting. His morning routine momentarily diverted by recall of the woman passenger, Professor Arecibo rises from his chair. At the window he adjusts the white microblinds and gazes far below to rain-scoured streets through which rush secrets and betrayals, perversity and longing.

A little later the secretary receives a call from the assistant and immediately forwards it to Arecibo's extension. Enthusiastically spilling his words, the young man says that the telescope managers have offered the professor a generous amount of research time on their big dish, which is located on another continent. Several complex issues regarding dates, equipment, and funding have been resolved, subject to the professor's approval. Then the junior colleague grunts, and Arecibo hears through the phone a series of staccato sounds and a loud, splattering splash.

"That's excellent," Arecibo says. "Good work."

"Thank you. But they've proposed new dates and some conditions. Do you want to take this down?"

More extraneous noises are coming through the receiver, pops and plops and slitherings, the whirl of water in displacement and gas and solids under pressure being released. Each acoustic evokes in Arecibo's imagination a vivid image of the unique, momentary physiological circumstance that has produced it. Muscles clench and interior chambers contract and dilate. The assistant sighs. Arecibo, who has for years patiently listened to the garrulous, electromagnetic universe for the whispered confidences of another intelligence, recalls now that the assistant often wears a mobile telephone headset.

"March fifth, 0600 to 0800, 1320 to 1420," the assistant says. "But they're not sure which peripherals will be available. March sixth, 0520 to 0720 . . ."

Arecibo suspects that the junior colleague resents him and that his ongoing sonata of excretory notes has been composed as a taunt. He isn't sure why he's resented, but presumes that the young man, a contributor to a recently well-received paper, considers himself the astronomy department's rising star, unappreciated by Arecibo, who in fact believes his self-confidence exceeds his capabilities. The assistant's show of disrespect is outlandish and also unprovable, so that Arecibo can never confront him or even complain about it to the chairman.

It's just as well that he can't complain, since it's possible that Arecibo has wrongly interpreted the call. As the meeting concluded, the assistant certainly knew that the professor was impatient for news, yet he urgently needed to use the lavatory. In not delaying his call, the assistant is perhaps being overconsiderate or overdedicated. He is an awkward young man, prone to gaffes and poor social judgment, as Arecibo once was. The sounds of each percussion and submersion now remind Arecibo of his own physiological indiscretions. He wonders whether he should judge the telephone call in a more generous spirit.

Arecibo assures his junior colleague that the details can wait until he returns, and in fact, why don't they review the meeting over lunch? The thought, however, repels him, especially after the assistant accepts the invitation with smooth alacrity, followed by a distant, echoing report. Arecibo renews his suspicion that, in receiving this call from the lavatory, he has accepted a covert insult.

When the conversation ends, Arecibo returns the receiver to the cradle and sits motionless at his desk, trying to keep himself from imagining how, in some other downtown office building, the junior colleague is now performing whatever final ablutions are required.

By the end of the day, which has comprised several small dramas and headaches, including the distasteful lunch date, Arecibo is feeling out of sorts. He leaves the university early and stops for a drink at a bustling commuter café near the central station. He finds a vacant stool at the bar and orders a Scotch and soda. When it arrives, he hunches over the tumbler, gazes into his drink, and takes a much-savored first sip. Then he looks up and sees his drawn, pale face in the wall-length mirror opposite the bar, alongside the faces of other men looming over their drinks. Fatigue also pallors the faces of the several women at the bar. He returns to his Scotch, intent on wringing from it every last molecule of relief.

"Professor Vladimir Arecibo."

He starts to turn, wondering who has found him. His name has been pronounced by the man on the adjacent stool, but when Arecibo opens his face to him, his eyebrows ascending toward a friendly expression, the man rotates too, away from him, making a show of guarding his privacy. He's speaking into a mobile phone. Embarrassed, the professor turns back to the bar and stares into the mirror. The man is a short, stout, bald fellow in a dark business suit: a complete stranger.

In a voice that seems incapable of finding a lower register, the man demands, "Is he returning today?" He hardly allows the other person to reply. "It's an urgent personal matter."

A number of patrons must have heard him speak the professor's name. The name is distinctive; it will lodge in their memories and they will carry it with them when they leave the bar and go out on the street and into the buses and trains that will take them to the city's other quarters, its suburbs, and beyond.

"Can I reach him on his mobile?"

Whomever he's speaking to declines to give him the number, suggesting to Arecibo that the other person on the line is the department's dependable, cautious secretary. She evidently asks for the caller's name and number, promising to pass it on. Nearly belligerent, the stranger complies but insists that she contact the professor at once.

Arecibo recognizes the man's name: someone he hasn't met, but a minor party in a slightly complicated and unfortunate situation involving Arecibo and another person. In an effort to impress the secretary with the call's urgency, the man begins explaining the situation in detail. The department secretary, who is Arecibo's friend and confidante, has already learned of this little imbroglio, but of course no one else at the bar has had the opportunity until now.

The professor furtively looks into the mirror at the other patrons. Some continue to drink or are involved in their own telephone conversations, but he believes he can detect from one end of the bar to the other signs of interest in the stranger's story, which is being delivered in a forceful voice apparently over the objections of the secretary, who is still promising to contact Arecibo right away. Heads turn to present their ears closer to the storyteller, and faces slacken as the audience gets caught up in the tale. It's lengthy, complex, and not without some humorous aspects, mostly at Professor Arecibo's expense. Sparks of amusement flicker across the other patrons' faces. Two women office workers pause in their chitchat. The aproned bartender stops wiping a glass. The narrative goes on to include the particulars of some appalling conduct, and Arecibo can see opprobrium reflected in the mirror as well.

The story is being told not entirely correctly, from Arecibo's point of view. He comes off as more petty, ignorant, and buffoonish than he really is. Nonetheless, in the hands of this raconteur it's an arresting anecdote, and Arecibo can imagine it repeated later in the evening or the next day, further corrupted to make him look even worse. In another drinking place or an office, in a restaurant or a bedroom, in an e-mail or a text message, or over another mobile phone, someone will say, "And the guy's name? It's Vladimir Arecibo!"

The man is about to make his final point to the secretary, a conclusion that will make it clear why Arecibo must call him back immediately. The professor now sees the story's destination: a completely unfair characterization of his predicament, but one that will provoke the most possible hilarity and revilement in listeners innocent of the facts. Even his secretary will reconsider the situation. Furthermore, although untrue in regard to the dilemma into which Arecibo has stumbled, the story inadvertently touches upon his most secret and shameful actual personal faults.

Trying not to draw attention to himself, Arecibo hurriedly slides off the stool and picks up his briefcase. He leaves some cash next to his glass. Another man takes his place. Arecibo flees the bar with the end of the story at his heels, and right behind it someone's snort of derision.

When he reaches the pavement, his phone vibrates in his inside jacket pocket, resonating deep within his chest and against his heart, down to its innermost chambers. The department secretary is calling. He takes out the device and hits its screen, demanding that it ignore the call. Around him men and women rush to their trains. At home they will huddle and confer, exchanging murmured intimacies. Arecibo will join them there, shortly, but as he prepares to hurl himself into the public maelstrom, it's with the fervent, inevitably frustrated desire to be alone, to know no one passing through the razor-sharp afternoon shadows of the city's blue-glass towers, no one threading his or her way across the car-choked terminal plaza, and no one entering the station's thunderous main hall. For a single deceptive moment, he's immersed in an interplanetary, interstellar, intergalactic silence.

INSTRUCTIONS FOR MY LITERARY EXECUTORS

1. The Big Book. If you look in the upstairs closet, behind where the storm windows are kept, you'll find a large Hefty bag, stuffed with about 4,000 sheets of paper. Some are blank, but many others contain unconnected fragments of prose. All my life I struggled to beach this whale of a novel, which dramatizes the universal themes of loss and redemption in a distinctly radical way, but I was never satisfied with the characters, the plot, the setting, or the point of view. Please tie together the most successful sections with whatever literary devices you find appropriate, adding story developments and protagonists only where strictly necessary, and publish. Set aside the extraneous material for future scholarship; relentlessly prohibit direct quotation.

2. Memoirs. I kept a journal every day of my adult life, through all these years of literary struggle and adventure. Regardless of whether I spent the day staring out the window or in line at the post office, I would turn every evening to my

notebook and record my thoughts. The journal consists mostly of one-word summaries of the weather and what I had for dinner; an industrious redactor will integrate them with daily newspaper reports to create a portrait of a man and his times. I've deposited the 184 marbled composition books in the vault of a Swiss bank with an impossible-to-remember name. I seem also to have misplaced the account number. You can ask the Swiss government for help.

3. Screenplay. Although I've been interested in cinema my entire life, originating some provocative ideas about the interplay of form and shadow, I never got around to writing a screenplay. Perhaps this had to do with my principled distaste for Hollywood. In any event, I've composed a few notes for a film treatment on a file card, which I put in a steel strongbox and tossed in the poured cement of the foundation of the new World Trade Center. The public may be ready for it now, especially if the cast includes Leonardo DiCaprio and Jennifer Lawrence. Please recover and develop, and ensure that the director (a hot indie?) films the gunplay, knife fights, and explosions in a thoughtful, balletic style. The Motion Picture Association of America may devise a special rating to allow the widest possible audience.

4. The Collected Correspondence. I was never much of a letter writer, but in the course of a long and varied literary life, I've left a lot of messages for people, mostly on their answering machines. Place a query in the *New York Review of Books*; certainly many of these answering-machine tapes have been saved and my messages can be retrieved from them. Don't edit the messages—please! I want posterity to "hear" me as I was. Also, my friends always enjoyed when I forwarded them "You Know You're Getting Old . . ." lists. Check their in-boxes and hard drives; publication of the jokes that I found humorous will provide insight into the more playful aspects of my character.

5. My Baseball Scorecards. Momentarily forgetting their terrestrial significance, I allowed these to be launched out of the solar system on board a NASA spacecraft. Recover them and you will find a fastidiously compiled record of every baseball game I ever attended. Most of these games seem to be 6–2 drubbings of the Mets. I suggest a facsimile edition with commentary on the games by, say, Thomas Pynchon. By the way, the score-keeping notation is entirely my own invention, but I'm sure some semiotician (Eco?) will look forward to the challenge of its exegesis for the ordinary reader who may or may not be a baseball fan.

6. Juvenilia. There are loads of this stuff—poems, limericks, school compositions, my summer-camp newspaper (annotate! annotate!)—mostly in a Yoo-Hoo chocolate-drink box in the basement, near the oil heater. A label, written in a nine-year-old's scrawl, reads, "Juvenilia," so it should be easy to find. Publish these pieces one at a time (with the suggestion that they've just been discovered) before bringing them out in a bound volume. The Library of America?

Thanks!